THE FOREST RANGER'S PROMISE

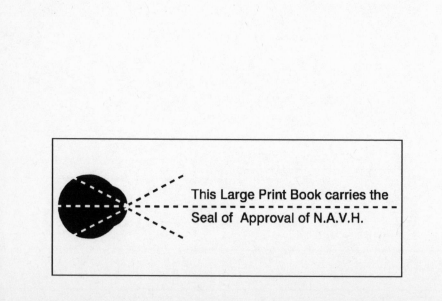

This Large Print Book carries the
Seal of Approval of N.A.V.H.

THE FOREST RANGER'S
PROMISE

LEIGH BALE

THORNDIKE PRESS

A part of Gale, Cengage Learning

Detroit • New York • San Francisco • New Haven, Conn • Waterville, Maine • London

GALE
CENGAGE Learning®

LIBRARY OF CONGRESS CATALOGING-IN-PUBLICATION DATA

Bale, Leigh.
    The Forest Ranger's promise / by Leigh Bale. — Large print ed.
        p. cm. — (Thorndike Press large print Christian fiction)
    ISBN-13: 978-1-4104-4432-5 (hardcover)
    ISBN-10: 1-4104-4432-5 (hardcover)
    1. Ranches—Wyoming—Fiction. 2. Ranchers—Fiction. 3. Wyoming—Fiction. 4. Large type books. I. Title.
PS3602.A59543F67 2012
813'.6—dc23   2011044247

Published in 2012 by arrangement with Harlequin Books S.A.

Printed in Mexico
1 2 3 4 5 6 7 16 15 14 13 12

But I say unto you, love your enemies, bless them that curse you, do good to them that hate you, and pray for them which despitefully use you and persecute you.

— *Matthew* 5:44

This book is dedicated to Dan Baird,
a genuine forest ranger and my hero.
Every child deserves a father like mine.

CHAPTER ONE

Thirty more minutes in the saddle and he could rest. Scott Ennison tightened his left hand around the reins, his stomach rumbling with hunger. The damp ground muffled the rhythmic beat of his horse's hooves. He breathed deep of the crisp July air, catching the sweet scent of sage and rain. You couldn't get this stunning beauty living in a city.

He looked up at the blue Wyoming sky and the jagged peaks of the Snyder Mountains. Farther out, a carpet of green pine led right down to the mouth of Game Creek where his truck awaited him. He'd be there soon and then on his way home. Shelley waited for him back in town, not at all happy that her daddy had left her with his office manager in a strange place. If only her mother were here. The divorce hadn't been easy on Shelley, not with his career. Living in small, remote towns. Being a single father raising a ten-year-old daughter on his own. Working all the time. Both of them lonely for their own separate reasons. No wonder Shelley was angry and missed her mom. She deserved so much more.

He redirected his thoughts, inspecting the hillside to check for erosion. After being in these mountains three days, he'd finished looking over the area. Now he had to decide how to proceed with a watershed study.

The rain that day would have chilled him to the bone if not for the heavy, down-filled coat he wore over his ranger uniform. He shifted his body and fanned his wet slicker over his arms. Even in July, the high mountains could be cold, especially after a storm.

As he pushed the forest ranger's hat back on his head, he scanned the thin trail ahead. It twined past several large, rotted tree trunks. A mass of pine needles, dried leaves and rotted bark lay in a pile next to the opening of one hollowed-out trunk. A large animal must have turned the tree over, grubbing for insects. He rode on, giving it no more thought.

Out of his peripheral vision, he caught a flurry of movement and turned in the saddle. Two bear cubs dashed across the carpet of damp leaves and scurried up a tall aspen. Scott's gelding jerked its head and jittered to one side.

A furious roar sounded from behind. Scott swiveled his head just as his horse bolted. The reins jerked from his fingers and he grabbed for something — anything — to keep from losing his seat. His fingers grasped empty air. He fell backward over the horse's rump. The ground slammed up to meet him. He landed on his back, the air whooshing from his body. Pain exploded at the back of his head. He lay there for several moments, dazed and hurting, gasping for breath.

Panic pumped through his body and he came to his feet, staggered and fell again. Pain choked off his breath and his lungs ached. As if in slow motion, he watched his horse race down the hill like a shot from a pistol. No more than fifty feet away, a grizzly bear stood on her hind legs. Using the aspens as a gauge, Scott figured she must be at least seven feet tall and weigh five hundred pounds.

Death stared him in the eye and all he could think about was Shelley. If he didn't make it home, she'd be all alone. No one to love and care for her. No one to keep her safe.

The bear's angry roar echoed off the surrounding mountains. Afternoon sunlight glimmered off her coarse, silver coat. White tips gave her fur a grizzled appearance. Scott had committed the unpardonable sin of coming between a mother and her cubs.

White-hot terror coursed through his veins. A rush of adrenaline forced him to his feet, but his vision swam like fog. He had to move. Had to run! But his legs wobbled and wouldn't obey his commands.

A shot rang out. Scott turned his head, trying to ignore the bolts of lightning tearing through his body with each movement. A woman sat atop her horse, the butt of a rifle braced against her right shoulder. He blinked, thinking he imagined her.

She cocked the rifle again and fired into the air. The bear screamed in fury. Scott flinched, his head pounding. He took a careful step in the woman's direction, his arms wide as he prepared to run. His head kept spinning and he stumbled, fighting to keep his balance.

The bear growled, her long, sharp teeth and claws extended. Waves of alarm washed over Scott. Another shot rang out. He stared in morbid curiosity as the sow lowered to all fours and dashed across the trail to her cubs. Her speed and agility surprised him. She got her cubs down from the tree, then swatted at them, herding them up the hill away from Scott and the loud boom of the rifle. That suited him just fine. Being eaten by a bear wasn't on his agenda today.

The cubs squawked in protest, but the sow growled and batted them, forcing them to continue up the mountain. Thankfully, her first priority was the safety of her cubs.

Scott faced the woman, shaking his head, trying to clear his blurry vision.

No, two horses and riders. A woman and girl. Where had they come from?

Scott's knees buckled and he lay flat on his back, gazing up at the sky. A biting chill blanketed his body. He couldn't fight it anymore. Something was wrong with him. He'd hit his head and couldn't focus.

Closing his eyes, he let the darkness sweep him away.

"I think he's dead, Mom."

Melanie McAllister kicked her mare. The animal zipped forward across the sage-covered field to join her daughter at the slope of the mountain. Lucky for the man, she and Anne had been out looking for stray sheep when they saw the grizzly bear. Reticent to kill a mother with cubs, Melanie had fired into the air, praying the bear didn't charge the man. She had never destroyed anything more than a bug and

13

she didn't want to shoot a full-grown grizzly bear. Since the animal was an endangered species, she could just imagine having to explain herself to a ranger.

"We'll check him, Anne. You stay close in case that bear returns, okay?"

"Yes, Mom."

The man's horse disappeared down the mountain. Melanie caught a glimpse of the roan gelding and didn't recognize the brand on the animal's hindquarters. The rain that morning had softened the ground, so it'd be easy to track the horse, if they had time. Right now, she had to think about the man and Anne's safety.

Anne had already hopped off her horse and knelt on the ground beside him.

"Wait, Anne! I told you to stay behind me." Melanie slid from the saddle before her horse came to a halt.

The man lay upon the damp grass, his long legs sheathed in green denim. His chest moved slightly, indicating life. Thank goodness.

His felt hat lay several feet away . . . a ranger's hat with a wide, flat brim. Melanie tensed, unable to deny her natural aversion to the Forest Service. Ranchers didn't like rangers. They just didn't, for lots of reasons. Mainly because the past few rangers stationed in Snyderville had rarely kept their promises and tended to tell the ranchers where and when to graze their livestock. Especially the last ranger, who'd practically been run out of town by an angry mob.

Melanie didn't recognize this man. He must be new. The rain slicker over his coat kept him dry. With his eyes closed, he looked harmless enough. A lock of sand-colored hair covered his high forehead. Thick eyelashes lay closed against sun-bronzed cheeks. Stubble covered his lean jaw and blunt chin. A handsome face in a stubborn, rugged sort of way. Definitely not a man who sat in an office all day. But it wouldn't matter if he was the best-looking man on earth. Not as long as he wore a green forest ranger's patch on the left shoulder of his shirt. This man meant trouble for Melanie — plain and simple.

"Is he dead?" Anne poked his arm with one finger, winning a soft groan from the fallen man.

"He's hurt." Melanie knelt beside her daughter and searched him for injuries. When she touched the back of his head, her fingers came away bloody. "He must have hit his head when he fell from his horse. Help me roll him over."

Anne grunted as she pushed against the

15

man's shoulder. A strand of auburn hair came free from her long ponytail. "He's big and heavy."

They got the stranger over on his side, so Melanie had better access to the gash in the back of his head. Without being asked, Anne ran to her horse and retrieved two bottles of water from her saddlebags. When she returned, Melanie popped the lid from one bottle, then removed the red-checkered kerchief she wore tied around her neck. She soaked it before cleaning the man's wound.

"Is he gonna die?" Anne asked. Her eyes filled with sadness. At the age of eleven, she'd already lost her father, and Melanie hated that her child had to grow up too soon.

"I don't think so, but he needs a doctor." She wouldn't lie to her daughter, even to protect her tender feelings. As sheep ranchers, they lived a hard life, surrounded by the death of some of their livestock every day, and Anne deserved the truth.

"Look, Mom. There's grizzly track all over this place. You think those bears will come back?" Anne pointed at a perfect indentation of a large animal's paw, the claws over three inches long.

Melanie sucked in a breath. "I hope they don't until we're gone."

Alarms sounded inside her head and she glanced at her .270-caliber rifle before scanning the trees for movement. In all the years she'd been grazing sheep on this mountain, she'd only seen grizzlies from a distance. She'd seen the damage they did to her sheep close up. As soon as they got down off this mountain, she'd report the sighting to the Wyoming Game and Fish Department. They'd send in professional trappers to catch and release the bears to a higher elevation.

Night was coming on, black and bitter. How was she going to get the stranger back to town? She knew from past experience that her cell phone wouldn't work here on the mountain, but she tried anyway. Flipping it open, she shook her head, wishing she could afford to invest in a satellite phone.

No reception. She and Anne were on their own.

She wouldn't take a chance with her daughter. She'd lost Aaron eleven months earlier, and she couldn't lose her little girl, too.

The man moved, lifting a hand to his face. "What happened?"

He rolled to his back, looking up at them, blinking his clear blue eyes in a daze. He tried to rise and she pressed her hand to his shoulder. "Just rest a moment and get your bearings."

"My horse — ?"

"We'll find him for you," Anne said.

The man closed his eyes and gritted his teeth. "My head feels like it's been split in two."

Melanie didn't laugh. Aaron had died from a similar accident, leaving her and Anne to fend for themselves with two bands of sheep. If only someone had been there to help Aaron, he might be alive now. That thought alone made her feel responsible for this man. He might have a wife and kids of his own and she was determined to do everything in her power to make sure that their father returned to them. "You hit a rock. You may have a concussion."

The man braced his big hands on the ground and tried to sit up. Melanie and Anne both reached to help him.

He groaned, rubbing his eyes. "My vision's blurry."

Melanie eyed him critically. "You sure you feel like sitting up?"

"Yeah." He closed his eyes again, then opened them. "There, that's better."

"You got a name?" she asked.

He swallowed, as if he felt nauseated. "En-

18

nison. Scott Ennison."

Melanie froze. Her heart felt as though it dropped to her feet. She'd never met this man, but she'd heard plenty about him from the other ranchers in the area. Scott Ennison, the new forest ranger over the Snyder District. The bane of every rancher's existence.

He wasn't what she expected. Ranchers had called the last ranger Overbellie because he was bald and fat and rarely went out on the range to see what difficulties the ranchers might be dealing with. But this man looked lean and strong, with a full head of hair and startling blue eyes.

"You're Ennison?" A look of repugnance crinkled Anne's freckled nose.

"Yeah, who are you?"

The girl stood and backed away, her hands resting on her hips. Dressed in denim and scruffy work boots, she looked every inch like her father. "I'm Anne Marie McAllister and you killed my dad."

Ennison blinked. "What?"

"Anne, don't say that. Your father's death was an accident. It wasn't anyone's fault." Melanie said the words mechanically, trying to believe them herself. It'd been Aaron's foul temper and drinking that had caused his death, not the forest ranger.

The girl's eyes narrowed with loathing. "You're good for nothing but causing us ranchers trouble."

"Anne!"

"Well, it's true." The girl whirled around and ran to her horse, burying her cheek against the warm side of the animal's shoulder.

Melanie stared after Anne, her heart aching. She understood her daughter's animosity, but didn't like Anne's disrespect and hateful words. Anne was too young to hate anyone. How she wished Aaron hadn't instilled a revulsion for rangers in their daughter.

Ennison's brow crinkled in confusion. "I don't understand."

Melanie wasn't about to explain. Not to this stranger. When she spoke, her voice sounded strained. "Do you think you can stand so we can get you on a horse? I think you need a doctor."

"Yeah, if you can just help me get down to the mouth of Game Creek, I've got a truck and horse trailer there."

"Okay." She preferred returning to her sheep camp. Game Creek was much closer, but if she didn't return, her herder might worry. As she helped Ennison stand, she noticed that Anne silently refused to lend a

20

hand. Something inside Melanie hardened. She also felt angry, yet it wasn't fair to blame this man for Aaron's death. Between the last ranger's dictatorial ways and Aaron's drunken rages, her family had suffered greatly.

Gossips in Snyderville said the previous ranger had lost control over the grazing permittees in the area. Even his kids were getting beaten up at school. The Forest Service claimed that Scott Ennison was an experienced range man from another district where he'd handled serious grazing problems. Ennison also had a reputation for being hardnosed, but fair.

Melanie would reserve judgment for now.

Since cattle and sheep men had a natural aversion to forest rangers, Melanie half wished she hadn't been the one to discover him. What would the other ranchers say when they found out she'd helped him? How would she ever live it down?

The story of the Good Samaritan filled her mind, reminding her that she should love her enemy and turn the other cheek. But no matter how hard she tried, she still didn't want to help this man.

Ennison walked steady, but once he sat in the saddle, he groaned and hung limp over the neck of Melanie's horse. Prickles of alarm dotted Melanie's flesh. What if he died? She didn't want any accusations flung her way.

"You okay?" She stood beside her horse, looking up at the man's pale face.

He straightened, his tall frame towering over her as he gave a weak smile. "Yeah, I'll be fine. I'm sure glad you showed up when you did. I think that mother grizzly had me on the menu for supper."

She almost chuckled, but couldn't bring herself to feel that comfortable around him. "I think it's time we left this place."

"I won't argue with you on that score."

She climbed up behind Anne on the girl's horse. Fearing Ennison might fall off his mount, Melanie took the reins, ponying him along beside her as they headed down the trail. They rode slow and steady and she glanced over her shoulder often to make certain Ennison was okay. She kept her rifle close at hand, just in case she saw a bear. Aaron had taught her to shoot. She'd chased off coyotes from her band of sheep by firing into the air. Aaron told her that did little good because they'd just return to steal sheep later on. He wanted her to shoot to kill, but she just couldn't, unless a person's life was at stake. Just like that mother grizzly, Melanie would do anything to protect her child.

As darkness covered the mountain, Melanie asked Anne to dig two flashlights out of her saddlebag. Aiming the beams of light at the trail, she silently prayed they didn't miss the turn leading to Game Creek.

Please, God, keep us safe tonight.

When they reached the camp, Melanie stared through the dark, just making out the Forest Service emblem with a lone pine tree on the side of Ennison's pale green truck. She breathed a sigh of relief. His horse stood beside the truck, its head up with reins trailing as it nickered gently in greeting.

"You knucklehead. Why didn't you take me with when you bolted?" Ennison asked the animal.

The horse just stared at them. Again, Melanie appreciated Ennison's humor and would have laughed if he'd been any other man.

It took thirty minutes to get the three horses loaded and Ennison settled in the front seat. Thankfully, the trailer was big enough to hold all the horses. No way was she about to leave her precious animals on this mountain alone. Not with grizzly bears prowling around. She depended on her horses for her livelihood and couldn't afford to buy new ones.

She and Anne climbed into the cab of the truck. The small overhead light came on. Ennison watched her quietly, his blue eyes clear and lucid. She didn't know how she'd ever live it down with the other ranchers if the new ranger died while in her care. Likewise, she doubted they'd let her forget helping him. In this small community, everyone knew everyone else's secrets.

"You know how to handle yourself with horses. You got those animals loaded in no time," Ennison commented.

She ignored his praise and stretched out her hand. "I need the key."

He reached inside his pants pocket and she heard the jingle as he placed some keys on her open palm. Anne sat hunched against Melanie's side, her lips pinched as she stared straight ahead and refused to let any part of her leg touch the man.

"I didn't catch your name," Ennison said.

"It's Mrs. McAllister." Melanie inserted the key and started the ignition.

"You don't have a first name?"

"Yes, I do." She turned on the headlights and put the truck in gear.

"What is it?" he persisted.

She tossed an irritated glance his way, finding the gleam of his eyes unsettling.

"Melanie, but my friends and family call me Mel. You can call me Mrs. McAllister."

She pressed on the accelerator, going slow. The horses thumped around in back, gaining their balance as the trailer bounced gently over the narrow dirt road.

"Wait a minute. You're Mel McAllister?" His eyes widened with surprise.

"That's right." She tried not to look at him, but found it difficult. Worrying about this man didn't sit well with her. She'd be a Good Samaritan this time, but that didn't mean she had to be friends.

"I recognize your name, but I thought you were a man."

She gave a harsh laugh. "Not hardly."

"I can see that."

Her cheeks heated up like road flares and she refused to look at him, grateful that the darkness hid her face.

"You're a grazing permittee," he said.

Her shoulders stiffened. "Unfortunately."

"You don't like grazing on the National Forest?"

"Of course I do. I just don't like being told when, where and how to graze my sheep."

She caught his nod of acquiescence. "I can understand your hostility, but believe me when I say I have nothing against grazing the land. It's here for us all to use." He sighed. "It's the overgrazing that I object to. That kills the land and causes erosion. With a bit of structure and management, there are ways to find a happy middle ground."

"Look, Mr. Ennison, my sheep aren't going to cause any harm to your precious land. I'm smart enough to figure out that if we overgraze we won't have enough quality feed for next year."

"It's not my land, Melanie. It belongs to everyone. I just want to help preserve it for future generations."

Her eyes narrowed. "I find that hard to believe."

"Oh, you can believe it. For every dollar generated by the use of our renewable natural resources, an income of ten dollars is generated somewhere else down the line." His voice filled with conviction. "Ranchers, auctioneers, loggers, truckers, the butcher in the grocery store, the contractor who builds our homes and many more — they all make a living because of our national lands."

She nodded. "I'm glad you understand that concept."

"Of course I do. We can't regrow an oil field, but we can regrow trees and raise more cows. Our renewable resources are highly important to our nation's economy." He smiled at her. "And, please, call me Scott."

Strike one. How dare he be so informal with her? She bit her lip to keep from telling him what she really thought. Who did he think he was? She knew very well how important the forest lands were to her own livelihood. "So you're not a preservationist?"

"I'm guided by the Multiple Use Sustained Yield Act, which tells me to take care of our land for use by the most people for as long as we can. Ranchers are an important part of that effort."

"Well. I'm glad we got that straightened out. But I'll have to watch and see if you act on your words." His ideas made sense and mirrored her own beliefs, but she'd heard other rangers say one thing and do another often enough not to trust what he said.

A low chuckle rumbled in his chest. "Just give me time, Mrs. McAllister. I'll show you I'm a man of my word."

She hoped so, but she wasn't certain she liked where this conversation was going. She could easily like this man, but she didn't want to. "Maybe I should have left you for the grizzlies."

He laughed, not seeming to be injured in the least by her harsh comment. "I'm glad you have a sense of humor. I think we'll get along just fine."

Was he daft? She had no intention of getting along with him. The sooner she got rid of him, the better.

"Don't think I'm easy pickings just because I'm a woman," she warned. "I know all the games you rangers play and I'm not falling for it ever again."

"Again?"

He studied her with those piercing eyes and she realized she'd said too much. The last thing she wanted was a snoopy forest ranger asking her questions.

"No games, Melanie. I grew up on a ranch myself. I know how important the land is to grazing livestock."

Hmm. Maybe so, but he was still a ranger and would undoubtedly do whatever his bureaucratic bosses told him to do. She'd learned the hard way not to trust a ranger and it wouldn't happen again.

CHAPTER TWO

It took an hour of slow driving to reach the main road. Melanie didn't head for Snyderville even to drop off her horses. Fearing Scott might die of some brain trauma, she sped on by the exit to reach the freeway to Evanston.

"Where you going?" he asked as they passed the road sign pointing to Snyderville.

Headlights blared in their eyes and she blinked as a semi passed them on the dark road. "I'm taking you to a hospital."

"That's ninety miles away."

"That's right," she said.

"There's no need for that. I'm fine."

"You may have a concussion and I won't be responsible for your death." She didn't look at him, wishing she could remain neutral. Wishing she didn't care. Her husband had always chided her for taking in strays. She never figured that might include an injured forest ranger.

Anne sagged against her in sleep, her bright head drooping to her chest. Melanie almost cringed when Scott reached over and settled the girl in a more comfortable position on the seat. His kindness annoyed Melanie and she didn't know why. His actions seemed too fatherly and she bit her tongue to keep from asking if he had kids. The less she knew about him the better.

She stared at the empty road, watching the miles go by, trying not to think of the man in the seat next to her. He filled up the truck with his bigger-than-life presence, so different from the previous ranger. This man was just too . . . likable.

The clock on the dashboard showed eight minutes past midnight when she pulled into the emergency parking lot in Evanston. She took up four parking spaces with the truck and trailer. Without a word, she climbed out and reached back to awaken Anne.

"Come on, honey. You can rest inside."

The girl stumbled out of the truck, almost knocking Melanie over. Scott startled her when he took Anne's arm to help. How did he get over here so fast?

"Leave me alone." The girl jerked away, her jaw hard with belligerence.

Scott drew back in surprise. "Sorry. I just

wanted to help."

Anne didn't smile and neither did Melanie. Anne had a natural aversion to men. She'd loved her father, but she'd also learned not to trust him. One minute, Aaron was fun and filled with gruff compassion. Then he'd lose himself in a bottle and became a mean drunk. Melanie had tried to shield Anne from her father's rages, but hadn't completely succeeded. The worst part about it was that Melanie now felt relieved Aaron wasn't around to hurt them anymore. She missed him even as she felt joy in his absence. How could a woman feel that way about her own husband? It just wasn't right and she felt guilty about it.

"Anne, don't be rude." Melanie led her daughter toward the lights of the hospital with Scott by their side.

In the brightly lit entranceway, he ran a hand down the back of his neck and Melanie sensed his deep frustration. She felt a nibble of guilt for being so curt with him but didn't dare let down her guard.

Inside, she sat with Anne on a blue sofa in the waiting room while he stepped up to the front reception counter. Like a mother hen, Melanie kept an eye on him, just in case he needed her. Whether she liked it or not, she was stuck in Evanston with no way home until Scott Ennison got checked out.

She wasn't certain what she'd do if the doctor decided to keep Scott overnight. Maybe she could drive his truck back to Snyderville without him and contact his office in the morning. His people could come out to her ranch to retrieve his truck and horse.

A nurse handed a clipboard with paperwork to Scott and he quickly filled it out before reaching in his pocket for his wallet and insurance card. An orderly glanced at Melanie. "Would your wife like to come back with you to the examination room?"

Melanie almost choked. "I . . . I'm not his wife."

"She's just a friend." Scott's blue eyes rested on her like a leaden weight. His gaze challenged her, as if he waited for her to deny his claim of friendship. The corners of his mouth curved slightly with amusement.

Melanie bit her tongue to keep from saying something rude and completely ruining all the good values she'd tried to instill in her daughter.

"Sorry. My mistake," the orderly said.

"Would you mind calling Karen Henderson?" Scott asked Melanie. "She's my office manager. Let her know what happened, but tell her I'm okay. I don't want to worry her."

"Sure." Melanie nodded and reached for her cell phone as Scott followed the orderly down the hall.

Melanie called information to get Karen Henderson's number, then made the call, keeping it short and sweet. Karen answered in a groggy voice and Melanie felt embarrassed. She had obviously woken Karen up, but there was no way around it. She quickly explained the situation, then hung up.

Sighing with exhaustion, Melanie wrapped an arm around Anne. She snuggled the girl close, breathing in her sweet smell before she leaned her head back.

Melanie would check on the horses in a few minutes. Right now, she felt absolutely worn out, her eyes gritty with fatigue. At least she had a clear conscience. Good Samaritan or not, God expected nothing less.

"You heard the doctor. I'm gonna be fine. I just have a mild concussion and a broken finger." Scott sat in the passenger seat, leaning his head back to rest while Melanie drove them home to Snyderville. He felt loopy from the pain medication, as if everything moved in slow motion.

Anne sat passed out between them, her small body hanging limp against her seat belt. Thick darkness covered the road, the headlights glinting off damp pavement as Melanie pulled onto the freeway.

Scott would have called his range assistant to come get him, but he figured by the time Jim got to Evanston, they could already be home. Instead, he'd woken up Karen again to let her know he'd be home by five in the morning. Until Scott could find another child care provider, Karen had agreed to take Shelley when he needed to work on the mountain. Something would need to change soon. Shelley was bored to tears, sitting all day in the office with a woman old enough to be her grandmother. No friends to play with. No mother to love her.

No wife to love him.

A sad melancholy settled over him. How he wished he could go back in time and change things. Shelley was the most important thing in his life and she was hurting. He'd have to find a better sitter on his next day off. That would go a long way toward mending Shelley's broken heart.

He doubted his own heart could ever be fixed.

"The doctor said you need to stay awake for a few more hours. Do you have family at home to watch you, to make sure you're okay?" Melanie asked.

No, but he didn't want to tell Melanie that. He could tell that she didn't want to be near him, but he knew she'd offer to stay with him if he needed her. He could hear the weariness in her voice and wouldn't ask that from her. "Yeah, I'll be fine."

"Did you call your wife and tell her what happened?"

Her voice had a low, growly quality he liked. Not a girly, simpering voice like so many other women he knew. Her assumption that he was married amused him. "My daughter will take care of me."

She flicked a glance of curiosity at him. "Is she old enough to watch you?"

He shrugged. "Probably not."

"That's just the point. You could be unconscious and unable to call for help. Who's at home? Is your wife out of town?"

He liked the note of concern in her voice. It'd been a long time since anyone cared about him. But her reminder that he had no one except his daughter made him feel a tad grouchy and he didn't understand why. "I'm divorced."

Now why did he tell her that? It wasn't her business. Must be the medication loosening his tongue.

"Oh. I didn't mean to pry."

He moved his left hand, careful not to jar

the broken finger and bulky splint the nurse had put on for him. Melanie's apology softened him as nothing else could. Over the past few years, it seemed he'd done all the apologizing. Now, he wanted to get on with life and forget his sadness. He'd resigned himself to raising Shelley and being alone. A ranger living in remote towns with few single women had little chance of developing much of a social life.

"It's okay. I guess you could say I chose my career over the needs of my wife. Not many women like living in podunk towns without a decent grocery store and shopping."

Once again, his tongue seemed to blurt out words before he could engage his brain. Melanie McAllister was much too easy to talk to.

Allison should be here now with him and Shelley. He'd begged his wife not to leave them. He'd even offered to change the career he dearly loved, although he had no idea what he'd do if he wasn't a ranger. This life was all he knew.

No amount of pleading had changed Allison's mind. She'd married a wealthy businessman less than four weeks after the divorce. All her trips to New York to visit her sister finally made sense. She'd been having an affair. When she'd claimed she'd never loved him, Scott wasn't surprised. Even now, the pain of betrayal hurt so much he thought there must be blood on the floor.

When she'd demanded that he keep Shelley, Scott had been glad, but his heart ached for his little girl. She didn't understand why Mom didn't want her anymore. He'd clumsily tried to explain without hurting her feelings, but Shelley was too smart. Kids had an uncanny way of guessing the truth. She knew her mother didn't want her. Had never really wanted either of them. And that's what hurt most of all.

"I suppose you're right," Melanie conceded. "It can be a challenge living in an isolated town, but we've got the most beautiful sunsets you ever saw. And when I'm up on the mountain after a rainstorm, the wind whispers through the trees and everything is so green and smells so fragrant. It's like heaven on earth."

Warmth and pride infused her voice. She spoke on a sigh, her soft words sounding poetic. He couldn't help wondering how different life might have been if his ex-wife had loved the great outdoors the way he did. They'd met and married fresh out of college, before he realized she hated country living. "It's funny how things change."

"Yes," Melanie said. "And it's funny how they stay the same, too."

How true. Right now, he wished he could just find some normalcy for himself and Shelley, if only for a while. They'd both had far too much upheaval lately.

"If your daughter's young, who's watching her while you're gone?" Melanie asked.

He explained about Karen. "Shelley's a great kid, but she's lonely. She misses her mom and her friends."

"Don't worry. There're several women in town who run summer child care out of their homes to make extra money."

"Yeah, for everyone except the new forest ranger." He couldn't keep the cynicism from his voice.

"I take it you've already asked them?"

"Yep, and each one said no."

"Really?" Disbelief filled her voice.

He snorted. "Don't look so surprised. One woman was polite, but I saw the anxiousness in her eyes when she found out who I was. The other two women bluntly told me they would never watch the forest ranger's brat."

She glanced at him, her eyes round with shock. "They actually said that?"

"Quote, unquote." And where did that leave him and Shelley? He'd never leave her with people who might treat her badly. His child care predicament bordered on desperate.

"I'm sorry. That's not very Christian-like." Melanie's mouth tensed as she gripped the steering wheel.

"Don't worry about it. Even you'd rather be anywhere but here helping me."

Her cheeks flamed with guilt. "Is it that obvious?"

"Like a fist punch to the nose."

"I don't mean to be rude," she admitted.

"I know. It's just that Shelley misses her mom and still doesn't understand why she has to live with me." His voice softened. "She's a lot like her mother. Prefers dresses to tromping around the mountains on a horse. But I love her so much. She's all I have left."

He heaved a deep sigh, then clamped his mouth closed. He must remember that this woman was a rancher and didn't trust him. Yet.

"I'm sorry for your trouble."

"Thanks. I just want to do a good job here," he said. "My dad died when I was a senior in high school and Mom couldn't keep the ranch going even with my help. We sold off our land and that's when I decided to get a college education, so I could become a forest ranger and help other ranchers. I'm really not an ogre."

She blinked, seeming to think this over.

"Can you recommend a child care provider until school starts up in the fall who won't care what I do for a living?" he asked.

She hesitated, then shook her head, her long auburn hair falling softly around her shoulders. "Just the women you've already tried. I pretty much keep to myself out at Opal Ranch and don't have time to mingle a lot with the townsfolk."

Something in her tone warned that he'd pushed her out of her comfort zone. She stared straight ahead, a frown curling the corners of her mouth. She didn't clarify, but he suspected there was a reason she didn't associate with the people in town and he couldn't help wondering why. For now, he decided to change the topic. "Opal Ranch is your home?"

"Yes, we're fifteen miles outside of town."

"How many bands of sheep are you running?"

"Two."

"With about four thousand head?"

"Closer to three." At his questioning look, she continued. "We've had some setbacks."

"Such as?"

"Such as nosy forest rangers," she retorted.

Wow! She was definitely harboring ill feelings toward the previous ranger. He could see he had his work cut out for him to resolve the anger issues in this town. Her clipped answers told him she didn't want to talk, but he should know this information as the new ranger. "How many acres of grazing land do you own?"

"Enough."

He smiled at the quirky way her full lips pursed together in disapproval. "I'm only trying to get to know your needs as one of the permittees. I just want to help."

"Are you laughing at me?"

He dropped the smile from his face, realizing she was dead serious. "Absolutely not."

"Good." She jutted her chin. "We have ten acres of corrals, eighty acres of hay land and another seventy acres of dry pasture, along with lambing and shearing sheds."

"Sounds like you have a busy operation."

"It's not a sideline, if that's what you mean. Some people come out here from the city, setting up a hobby ranch so they can play with the sheep and cows. For my family, it's our livelihood and our way of life. My family has owned Opal Ranch for generations. It would kill me to lose our land and —" She clamped her mouth closed, as if realizing she was telling him too much.

"I understand."

She glanced at him, a doubtful frown creasing her brows. "Do you really?"

"Yes, I do. Really. You don't like me very much." He shouldn't have said that. He'd always been too direct. Allison never liked that aspect of his personality. He called things as he saw them, but Allison preferred to play silent, sulking games. He'd never known a person who could hold a grudge as long as Allison.

Melanie glanced at him, her green eyes shooting daggers. "If you were me, would you like the ranger very much?"

"Sure. I'm a nice guy and I've never done anything to hurt you."

She took a deep, exasperated breath before letting it go. "Surely they told you the problems stirred up by the last ranger here in Snyderville?"

"They?" he asked.

"Yeah, your bosses. The people you work for. They must have told you about the trouble the last ranger caused."

"Yes, that's why they brought me in. To help smooth all of that over."

She snorted. "And how do you intend to do that?"

"One permittee at a time. I thought I'd start with you."

"No." She shook her head, staring straight ahead.

"You don't even know me."

"I think that's best," she said.

"And yet you helped me."

"Wouldn't you have done the same?" She tilted her head to look at him, her delicate features outlined in shadows. She seemed too dainty to be running a sheep ranch, and he got the impression she made up in spirit what she lacked in physical strength.

"Of course I would." He met her eyes. "What did the other ranger do to upset you so much?"

"For one thing, he made a lot of promises he never kept."

"I won't do that. Not ever." And he meant it.

"We'll see."

He sighed, realizing it would take time for him to prove himself.

She squirmed in her seat. "Look, can we change the subject?"

"Sure. What do you want to talk about?"

She didn't bat an eye. "How old is your daughter?"

"Almost eleven."

"My Anne is eleven."

He peered through the darkness at the sleeping girl, finding her mouth open slightly as she breathed. She looked like a sweet child. A smaller version of Melanie, with a pert nose and cheeks sprinkled with freckles and auburn hair like her mom's. "What grade is she in?"

"She'll start sixth grade in the fall."

"Shelley will be in the sixth grade, too. Maybe they can be friends."

Melanie looked doubtful and then he remembered Anne's accusation on the mountain. "Why does Anne blame me for her father's death?"

Melanie sucked in a deep breath.

"Oh, I'm sorry," he added. "Is that getting back into a taboo subject?" He tried to tease her, to lighten things up a bit, but the look on her face told him it wasn't working. He saw something in her eyes, something vulnerable and fearful. From the little he knew about this woman, he realized she'd been hurt and he sensed the pain went deeper than just the loss of her husband. What had happened to her?

She licked her top lip, seeming to choose her words carefully. "Let's just say the last

44

ranger wasn't a nice man and let it go at that."

Her revelation made Scott's mind run rampant. He'd never met Ben Stimpson, but he'd heard that the man used some illegal threats to force the ranchers to do his bidding. Had Stimpson threatened Melanie?

Scott sensed a deep reticence in her words. Once her husband died, Ben could have helped Melanie and her daughter, making their lives much easier. Or he could have made things more difficult. Scott figured from Melanie's comments that it had been the latter.

They didn't speak much over the next few miles. When she pulled into Snyderville, he breathed a sigh of relief. One lonely streetlight guided their way down Main Street. The morning sun had just peeked over the eastern mountains and he was grateful they were all home safe.

Karen, her husband, Mike, and Scott's range assistant, Jim Tippet, were all at his house to meet him. As Melanie pulled into the gravel driveway, they came outside fully dressed, Jim's thinning hair sticking up in places.

"Thank goodness you're home. Are you okay?" Karen asked as she rushed over to

45

take Scott's arm.

"I'm fine, thanks to Mrs. McAllister." Scott smiled at Melanie, who stood back with her arms folded. Anne continued sleeping in the truck.

Jim looked at Melanie. "Good thing you were up on the mountain and found him when you did."

A tight smile curved her lips. "I was glad to help."

Yeah, right. Scott doubted her words, but he respected her for doing the right thing in spite of her dislike for him. Without her and Anne, he'd probably be dead now.

"Let me unload Tam and I'll put him in the corral before I drive Mrs. McAllister home." Jim went to retrieve Scott's horse.

"I'll help you," Mike said.

As the two men rounded the back of the horse trailer, Scott looked at the Forest Service house, painted white with green trim. Someone had turned the porch light on. Even though he had kind people here to help, he felt overwhelmed by loneliness. "Where's Shelley?"

"Inside sleeping. She doesn't even know anything happened," Karen said.

"Good. I didn't want to frighten her." No matter what, he wanted to protect his daughter and let her have as normal a childhood as possible.

"Let's get you inside so you can rest," Karen urged.

Scott reached out his hand to Melanie. "Thank you, Mrs. McAllister. I owe you."

Melanie hesitated before shaking his hand. Her fingers felt chilled and delicate against his.

"You don't owe me a thing," she said.

Scott watched her return to the truck, sliding in beside her sleeping daughter. Injured and alone on the mountain without a horse, he could have died. He had Melanie to thank for his life. Right then, he decided he would do everything in his power to return the favor.

As Karen led him up the front steps to his house, he stared at the front door. Thinking about the big, empty rooms, he wished he didn't have to go inside. If only he had someone to come home to each night besides Shelley. Someone who loved and cared for him as much as he cared for her.

CHAPTER THREE

"Why do we have to come here, Dad? I wanna go home." Shelley crinkled her nose with repugnance as Scott rapped his knuckles on the front door of the redbrick house.

White trim surrounded each sparkling window. The front porch circled the house, with white paint peeling along the slim columns supporting the second floor. The front gate stood ajar, sagging on its hinges. Cracked cement along the foundation showed a lack of care. Several boards hung loose on the toolshed at the back edge of the lawn. Everything looked tidy, but repair jobs had been ignored. It occurred to him that Melanie McAllister might need his help as much as he needed hers.

"Shell, I've already explained to you three times," he told his daughter. "The people living here saved my life. The least we can do is thank them."

The girl released an exaggerated sigh.

"All right."

Opal Ranch. Jim had told Scott that the ranch had been named for the white and gold mountains surrounding the valley. Poplars lined the long gravel driveway. Scott remembered Melanie talking about the beautiful sunsets and he could understand why she loved it here. As the summer breeze blew through the treetops, he envied the beauty and solitude of this place.

Shelley peered at the open fields of hay and alfalfa. Boredom crinkled her brow. She stood beside him wearing a short white skirt and sandals, her long, blond hair pulled back with a pink ribbon. Delicate and pretty as a picture.

She held a paper plate of homemade chocolate chip cookies covered with tin foil. Thinking it might be quality time together, he'd insisted that she help him make the cookies after he took two aspirin for his pounding headache. She'd sat on a kitchen stool and munched chocolate chips while he mixed the dough. No amount of cajoling could get her to help measure out the flour and eggs.

"Why couldn't you just call to say thank you?" the girl complained.

"You wanted something to do. We're doing something right now." He forced a smile, her grumbling getting on his nerves. In addition to her pretty looks, she'd inherited her mother's penchant for whining. He hoped to change that someday soon.

"Maybe no one's home." A hopeful lilt filled her voice.

"Maybe they're working out back." Scott peered at the rusty old truck sitting in the driveway. He let go of the screen door and it clapped closed. His booted heels pounded the wood as he walked the length of the porch. He ducked his head so he wouldn't hit the hanging baskets of white petunias and blue lobelia. Several large clay pots filled with white, fragrant alyssum sat along the edge of the porch and he breathed in deeply. Having a background in botany, he was probably one of the few regular men in the world who knew these names.

He glanced around with interest. The green lawn showed impeccable grooming, with flower beds of tall hollyhocks. A vegetable garden of peas, lettuce and beets filled the backyard, guarded by a white picket fence. No tomato or pepper plants. Scott knew they wouldn't grow well at this cooler elevation.

It seemed Melanie had a green thumb and he liked that for some odd reason.

Shelley followed him, hanging back as a

black-and-white border collie with droopy ears trotted out of the barn. The animal gave one bark, then greeted them by sniffing their legs.

"Will he bite?" Shelley circled her dad, seeking protection.

"I don't think so." Scott leaned forward and put out his hand, letting the animal sniff him. Considering they were strangers, the dog seemed composed and gentle. Most likely one of Melanie's sheepdogs, trained to be calm and not bark a lot.

"Hi there, fella. Where's your master?" Scott scratched the dog's ears.

"Probably in the barn," Shelley said.

"Hello! Anyone here?" Scott stood at the back of the McAllisters' house and shouted. He gazed at the variety of green fields, lean-to's for working in the hot sun, barns, sheds and corrals filled with sheep. Low fences with tight rails and netting kept the sheep from squeezing through. A tractor, four-wheelers and other equipment sat parked neatly at the side of the garage. Melanie could be anywhere, even up on the mountain. He figured that since they'd been up all night at the hospital, she would have had a late start, like him, and stayed home to work today.

"Dad! Look at the babies," Shelley exclaimed, pointing at a corral where approximately thirty small lambs scampered around, bawling for their mothers.

"Come on." Scott stepped off the porch and headed across the road leading to the barn. The dog trotted beside them, its tongue lolling out of its mouth as it panted. The stench of animals filled the air.

"Yuck! It stinks here." Shelley pinched her nose.

"Breathe through your mouth instead of your nose. You'll get used to it," Scott advised.

The girl gave him a look of incredulity, which he ignored. It had been tempting to leave Shelley with Karen today, but he knew they'd never become close that way. The sooner Shelley got used to living in Snyderville, the happier she'd be. Which would make him happy.

He hoped.

At the corrals, Shelley stood on the bottom rail of the fence, holding the plate of cookies as she leaned over the top rail to peer at the little, fluffy lambs. He hoped she didn't drop the plate.

"Oh, they're so cute. Can we play with them?"

Scott chuckled. "I thought you didn't want to come along. You thought this would be boring."

She showed a grin of slightly crooked teeth. "That was before I knew we were gonna see sweet little babies."

Victory! He'd finally found something she liked.

"Come on. Let's see if anyone's here. Maybe you can play with the lambs." He inclined his head toward the barn.

The wide double doors stood open, the bright sunlight filtering inside. As Scott stepped into the shadows, he caught the pungent aroma of straw and animals. Dust motes floated in the air. Stalls lined one wall of the barn with a small tractor, shovels and other tools hanging neatly on hooks along the other wall. He heard voices coming from the opposite end of the barn.

"You think she's too tender to ride?"

"Nah, she'll be all right. Won't you, girl?"

Scott followed the voices, hearing several muted clapping sounds, as if someone were patting a horse.

Conscious of Shelley hovering at his heels, he peered into a stall at the far end of the barn. An older man wearing a beat-up Stetson and a white, scruffy beard stood bent over a mare's right front leg. The man held the animal's hoof between his knees. Wearing baggy, faded blue jeans and old cowboy boots, he used a metal pick to clean dirt away from the sole of the horse's hoof. He grunted as he fought to reach over his own rotund belly.

Melanie stood leaning against the stall, one booted foot raised and braced against the wooden wall behind her. Her forehead crinkled and her delicate jaw tensed as she watched the farrier work. Strands of auburn hair came free of her long braid, resting against her flushed cheeks. Even wearing blue jeans, she looked too feminine for such work, but Scott knew better. Life couldn't be easy with her husband gone, but this woman had spunk and was sure of what she was doing. Scott couldn't help admiring her.

"See here?" The farrier pointed at the hoof and Melanie lowered her foot as she leaned forward to see. "I'll rasp the outside of the heel, but not the inside toe, which is much lower. I think once we get the heels lined up with the back of the frog, she'll be in good shape for riding."

Scott took a step and Melanie turned, her green eyes widening. His senses went into overdrive the moment she looked at him. Since when had he had such a reaction to a woman? Even Allison never made him feel warm and gushy inside. He rubbed one hand over his face, regaining his composure.

Her gaze lowered to his drab olive Forest Service shirt and the badge he wore on the flap of his left front shirt pocket. Her lips pursed together in annoyance. Casting a quick glance over her shoulder at the farrier, she pushed a curl of hair back behind her ear. "Mr. Ennison. This is a surprise." She gestured nervously toward the bearded man. "Have you met Pete Longley? He's a local rancher and the best farrier around Snyderville."

"I've heard your name. Glad to meet you." Scott extended his right hand.

Pete let go of the animal's hoof and stood straight before clasping Scott's hand. "Howdy."

Melanie fidgeted with a bridle hanging on a hook by the stall gate. "Umm, Mr. Ennison's the new ranger in town."

"That so?" Pete let go of Scott's hand a bit too abruptly and narrowed his gray eyes. He studied Scott for several moments before he turned and spat into the dirt. And just like that, Pete dismissed him.

The shaggy man didn't say another word as he went back to his work on the horse, but his actions spoke volumes. Scott knew the drill and had become inured to this attitude. Pete didn't respect him simply because he was the forest ranger. He'd find another opportunity to chat with the man later, but right now, he wanted to talk to Melanie.

"What did you want?" she asked.

Shelley peered around his back and Scott pulled his daughter forward. "I never really got to say thank you last night, so Shelley and I made cookies for you."

Melanie crinkled her brow in confusion. Shelley held out the plate, a shy look on her face. Melanie flashed such a bright smile that Scott sucked back a startled breath and stared. Melanie bent slightly at the waist so she could look Shelley in the eye. "You made these cookies?"

"Yeah, Dad and me." Shelley tossed a sheepish smile at her father as Melanie took the plate. He hoped that this was a step in the right direction. If Shelley saw how their offering pleased Melanie, perhaps she might learn something about service to others. Normally Scott would have settled for store-bought cookies, but he was trying to be both a mother and father to his daughter. Though Melanie seemed to hold animosity toward him, Scott felt relieved that she treated his daughter with kindness.

He noticed Pete casting speculative glances his way. In return, Melanie shifted her weight to block Pete's view.

Scott could take a hint. Neither Melanie nor Pete wanted him here, but Scott had been selected for this job for a good reason. It'd take time, but he was determined to work with these ranchers and clean up the problems his predecessor had left in his wake.

"Thank you. I'm sure Anne will gobble them down. I'd better hide them until after dinner," Melanie said.

"Who's Anne?" Shelley asked.

"My daughter. She's out in the sheds feeding the lambs. She's just about your age."

"I'm almost eleven."

"Your dad told me. Anne just turned eleven last week." Melanie pointed at the door. "You can go see the lambs if you like. They're awfully sweet."

Shelley's face lit up with eagerness. "Can I, Dad?"

Thank goodness. He'd begun to wonder if she'd ever find anything pleasant about Snyderville.

"Sure, honey. Just be careful."

Shelley trotted off, excited to play with the lambs. It'd be great if she made a new friend and took some interest in their new life here. Scott watched her go with mixed feelings. He hadn't seen her this animated

57

since they'd moved to Snyderville three weeks earlier. He'd never expected her to find such pleasure at the McAllister ranch. Considering how she could have reacted, Melanie had been surprisingly civil to his daughter and Scott appreciated it more than he could say.

"So did you need anything else?" Melanie asked, urging him toward the barn door.

Scott would have left, but he also had a job to do. He wasn't about to let this woman rancher with a kind heart chase him off. Not until he won her over and found a way to help her with her grazing permits.

"Actually, I wanted to ask you something."

They stepped outside and he enjoyed a breeze that cooled the sweat on his brow and neck. He felt incredibly lucky to be alive. Because of Melanie, he had a second chance at happiness. His experience with the grizzly had changed him somehow, renewing his appreciation for life. He didn't want to take anything for granted, especially Shelley.

"What's up?" Melanie asked, resting her hands on her slim hips. Sunlight glinted off her hair, showing deep highlights of brown, red and gold. Like fire on the mountain. He almost reached out to touch it.

"I'd like to make a personal business arrangement with you."

Her eyes narrowed with suspicion. "What kind of business arrangement?"

He indicated the picket fence with his chin. "I can see you need some help around this place and I need summer child care. How would you feel about watching Shelley for me during the weekdays and in return I'll work for you on the weekends and some evenings?"

As he expected, her mouth dropped open and she stared as if he'd gone daft. She cleared her throat and studied the barn, thinking things over.

"Shelley's a good girl," he hurried on. "She wouldn't be much trouble. In fact, she can help you with chores. And I've taught her to ride. She'd do fine, if you gave her a gentle horse."

He was talking fast now, hoping she'd agree. Hoping she'd look past his position as the forest ranger and see that they could help each other out.

Melanie whirled around and looked him in the eye. "Why would you ask me to do this? I'm basically a stranger. You don't really know me, yet you're willing to leave your child with me?"

He nodded. "Karen told me you're a good, hardworking woman. She said you'd take care of Shelley, but keep her busy so she didn't have time to whine about how much she hates leaving her old friends." He smiled. "Besides, any woman who would help me the way you did last night couldn't be bad. I already feel as if I've known you for years."

Maybe he shouldn't have said that, but it was true. He felt more comfortable around Mel McAllister than around any woman he'd ever met. She wasn't afraid to get her hands dirty and she didn't worry about mussing her long hair.

Karen had also told him that Melanie's husband had been an alcoholic, which was one reason Opal Ranch wasn't doing so well. When Scott heard this, he understood why Melanie didn't mingle with the towns-folk much. When your husband was a drunk, you didn't have many friends. Having grown up with an alcoholic father, Scott would never forget the drunken rages, financial destitution, teasing from other kids and feelings of fear and abandonment. Melanie had a good reason not to trust others.

Melanie chuckled, a low, raspy sound. "I take it Shelley's not too pleased that her dad dragged her here to Snyderville?"

"Nope. Not pleased at all." He smiled, feeling oddly happy to be talking to this woman. Being near her was the highlight of his day.

"Well, a friend might do my Anne some good, and I could sure use your help around this place." She hesitated, wrapping her arms around her waist. The action made her seem vulnerable and he was struck by a sudden desire to protect her.

"So it's a deal?" he urged.

"Okay, we'll try it for one week. If the girls don't get along or it's not working out, you'll have to take Shelley somewhere else. Agreed?"

"Agreed."

She gave him a smile so bright he had to blink. It lit up her face and softened her eyes and he thought he'd never seen anything so beautiful in all his life.

What was wrong with him?

He coughed and looked away. "Now that's settled, I've got one more question for you."

"Okay." Her green eyes looked guarded.

"Anne said something yesterday that's been bothering me."

"What's that?" Melanie prodded.

"She blamed me for her father's death."

Melanie rubbed her ear before taking a deep breath and exhaling. "Please don't hold that against her. She's still hurting over her dad's death and doesn't trust men very much."

"But why would she blame me?" Scott spoke gently, trying to be sensitive to their loss. Trying to understand.

"It was an accident. Ben Stimpson warned Aaron to move our sheep, but Aaron wouldn't listen."

"Ben Stimpson, the previous ranger?"

Melanie nodded. "I didn't know until after the accident that Aaron was grazing illegally on the forest. He moved one of our bands of sheep onto the grazing allotment twenty days early and Stimpson told him to move them or he'd have them moved for us. Stimpson said he'd sell them to pay the fine."

Scott would have done the same, after one fair warning with enough time to move the sheep. "So what happened?"

She shrugged one slim shoulder. "Aaron wasn't in any shape to move the flock. He . . . He'd been ill and went out during a thunderstorm."

From Melanie's hesitation, Scott couldn't help wondering if Aaron McAllister had been drunk that night.

"I begged him to wait until the next day when some of our men could have helped, but we couldn't afford to pay another fine.

He was angry and wouldn't listen to reason. Our herder found him the next morning. It wasn't anyone's fault. It was an accident." Emotion thickened her words and she turned away, brushing at her eyes.

Scott longed to comfort her, but realized now wasn't the time. Compassion settled in his chest. She'd obviously loved her husband and he couldn't help wishing someone felt that way about him.

He shifted his weight and leaned against a fence post. "So now Anne blames the forest ranger — any forest ranger — for her dad's death."

Melanie's mouth tightened, her eyes filled with sadness. "Yes. He died from a broken neck. His horse had a broken leg and had to be put down. We figure the animal stumbled or lightning spooked it. We'll never know for sure." She sighed heavily. "If Aaron had waited until morning, we would have had to pay a hefty fine . . . but he'd still be alive."

"And what about Ben Stimpson?" He hated to push her, but longed to know exactly what the other ranger had done to spook her.

Her spine stiffened. "What about him?"

"Did he fine you for the sheep, even

though your husband died trying to move them?"

Angry tears filled her eyes. "He was going to, but that's when several men wearing ski masks paid him a visit in the middle of the night and threatened him. He and his family left town the next day."

Something cold clutched at Scott's heart. He figured Stimpson deserved to be chased out of town, but the thought of masked men coming to his house in the middle of the night and terrorizing Shelley didn't sit well with him. "Who were the men?"

"I don't know their identities, but as far as I'm concerned, they were my guardian angels."

Her voice cracked and so did his heart. Scott sensed that she'd reached deep inside herself to tell him these things. Private feelings she probably hadn't shared with many people. He wasn't about to take her admissions lightly.

"I'm sorry, Melanie." What else could he say? It wasn't anyone's fault Aaron died; it just happened. But that didn't make Scott feel any better about the way Stimpson had treated the McAllisters.

"Anne's just a child. One day, she'll understand about her father," Melanie explained.

Scott had doubts. "Traumatic events can scar children so they never forget. Shelley hasn't said so, but I sense that she blames me for my divorce from her mom."

He regretted his failings and wished more than anything that Shelley would forgive him.

Melanie gave a hoarse laugh. "It seems that you're bearing the brunt of everyone's blame these days."

"I guess so." He chuckled, the sound low and rumbly. Inside, he ached with regret.

"I didn't mean to unload on you," she confessed. "You're the last person I should confide in."

And yet, she had. Somehow it made him feel close to her, and he'd sworn never to get close to another woman again. Especially not a widowed rancher whose young daughter hated him.

Remembering his job and his purpose here in Snyderville, he stepped back. He must keep his relationship with Melanie McAllister completely professional. He had no room for friendship or romance in his life right now. He had to remember that.

"You shouldn't be in here." Anne eyed the strange girl as she stepped into the shadows of the lambing shed.

The black-and-white dog followed Shelley inside, and Anne pointed at the door while speaking in a stern tone. "Get out, Bob. You know you're not supposed to be in the lambing sheds."

Used to responding promptly to orders, Bob obeyed without even a whine.

Anne frowned when the girl didn't turn and follow the dog out. "Who are you?"

"I'm Shelley. Your mom told me to come and help you feed the baby lambs."

Anne stared at the girl's long, bare legs, white sandals and blue-painted toenails. Maybe Mom would let her buy some blue nail polish the next time they went shopping in Evanston. All she had was pink and red. "You can't feed lambs dressed like that."

"Why not?" Shelley stepped backward into a pile of manure. Crinkling her nose with repugnance, she wiped her sandal off on a clean bed of straw before moving to stand over by the wall.

Anne shook her head in disgust, figuring she didn't need to point out the obvious. "Where'd you come from?"

"My dad and I brought your mom a plate of chocolate chip cookies."

That sounded nice. Cookies were okay with Anne. "Do you have sheep?"

Shelley shook her head. "No, but I have a cat named Wilson."

Strange name for a cat. "Who's your dad?"

"Scott Ennison."

Anne scowled. She should have known. "You shouldn't be back here."

"Why not?"

" 'Cause we're enemies."

Shelley's eyes widened. "We are?"

"Yes. You're Forest Service and I'm a rancher. Don't you know anything?"

"I'm not Forest Service. I'm just a kid."

"It doesn't matter," Anne scoffed. "Your dad's the ranger."

"So? Can't we still be friends?"

Anne glared at her. "Of course not."

"Why not?"

Anne searched her mind for a valid reason that didn't sound childish. She tried to remember why her dad hated forest rangers so much, but he'd never really told her his reasons. Just that they forced him to graze his sheep where he didn't want to graze them. Anne had hated it when Dad drank from his bottle because he got even angrier at the ranger. One time she had even climbed up the cupboard and hidden Dad's bottle so he wouldn't drink anymore. When he found it missing, he'd blamed Mom and slapped her across the face. Mom must have known it had been Anne who had taken the bottle, but she never said a word. Mom's face and lips had been swollen for a week, making Anne feel guilty. Even now, she missed Daddy more than she could say. If he'd just come back home, she'd promise never to hide his bottle again.

When she realized that Shelley was still waiting for an answer, Anne shoved away the painful memories and faced her nemesis. "Your dad bosses my mom around."

"You're a liar. My dad's nice. He helps ranchers."

Anne pursed her lips when she saw the ugly glare on the other girl's face. She didn't want to fight with this stranger. Mom would find out and then she'd be in big trouble. "We'll see."

Shelley shrugged, then bent over to pet the fluffy wool of a two-month-old lamb. The little animal hurried by to get at the stalls where Anne was setting up the feeder. Eight pens divided the shed. Anne set out bottles with rubber nipples on a feeding rack, then opened the gate and brought in seven little lambs one at a time. The babies nuzzled up to suckle. One zipped past Shelley, its tail wagging like a whirling dervish as it latched on to a bottle with ferocity. Shelley gave a startled yelp.

"You don't need to be afraid of them. They're just hungry," Anne said. "Haven't you ever petted a lamb before?"

"No. They're so soft." Shelley's eyes gleamed with happiness as she rubbed a lamb's velvety ears.

"What are you, a city kid or something?"

Shelley shrugged, looking out of place in her girly skirt. Anne couldn't help envying the other girl's creamy complexion and blond hair. She figured Craig Eardley would pay more attention to her if she had Shelley's blue eyes. Instead, Anne had bright red hair she kept pulled back in a ponytail, green eyes and freckles all over her face, even on her forehead. She could kick the ball off the blacktop at school and run fast, but the boys never chased her during kissing tag. She figured they'd chase after Shelley, though.

"What are their names?" Shelley asked.

"You can't name them," Anne scolded.

"Why not?"

"Because we sell and eat them. Sheep are a cash crop. Don't you know anything?"

Okay, that wasn't entirely true. Mom told Anne not to name the lambs so she wouldn't be sad if one of them died or if they sold them, but Anne did it anyway. Just a few of her favorite lambs.

"You eat them?" Shelley's blue eyes widened with horror.

Anne laughed. "Nah, not really. Mom says we don't eat our sheep. We just raise them for wool."

"Oh, okay." Shelley smiled with relief, bending over to snuggle one sweet, fuzzy lamb.

Anne didn't want to like this girl, but she couldn't help it. Shelley didn't know much, but she seemed to love the lambs as much as Anne did. Obviously, Shelley needed someone to teach her what to do on a sheep ranch.

"Where're their mothers?" Shelley asked.

"They don't have moms. These are dogie lambs. They're orphans."

"Doggie lambs?"

"No, you're saying it wrong. They're not doggie lambs, like Bob is a dog. You say it like *dough.* Dough-gie lambs."

Shelley repeated the word perfectly.

"Yeah, that's what orphans are called."

"Oh, that's so sad." Shelley hugged the lamb again as it tugged on the bottle.

Anne waved a hand in the air. "They're okay. We take good care of them. They're already nibbling hay and alfalfa pellets. Soon, we'll be taking them out to graze in the paddock."

The hungry lamb jerked, knocking Shelley back into the straw. The girl laughed. "What happened to their moms?"

"Some died, but sometimes the ewe has twins or triplets and she can only take care of one or two of her babies when she goes up to the summer pasture to graze. So we bring the smaller baby here to tend."

"Then not all the moms died?"

"Of course not, silly." Anne snickered. "You really don't know much."

"Then I guess I'm a dogie lamb, too."

Anne raised her brow. "What do you mean?"

"My mom isn't dead, but she doesn't want me. My dad doesn't think I know, but I do."

Shelley sounded like she was about to cry. Anne felt like crying, too, but refused to let it show. Even when Dad had been alive, she'd had an empty feeling inside all the time. Like he didn't really love or want her. Like he preferred his bottle to her and Mom. But she'd always had Mom to love her. How horrible not to be wanted by your own mother. "What mom doesn't want her kid?"

Shelley scuffed a sandaled foot against the rough lumber of the feeding stall. "Mine doesn't. She got married to Malcolm Henley the third, and he doesn't like kids, so I have to live with Dad. I heard them arguing about it late one night when I was supposed to be asleep." A glimmer of a smile touched her lips. "Dad can't cook much, but at least he wants me. He got this new transfer to Snyderville and I had to leave all my old friends behind."

Anne thought this over for a moment, biting her lower lip. Shelley didn't have any friends, just like her. During recess, the kids at school called her the town drunk's daughter and she'd learned to play by herself. "Then that makes you half a dogie because you still have your dad. I guess I'm a half dogie, too. My daddy died, but I still have Mom and she loves me lots."

Tears glistened in Shelley's eyes. "My dad loves me, too. I'm sorry we're both half dogies."

"Me, too."

And right then, Anne knew it wasn't Shelley's fault that her father was the forest ranger. They had a lot in common. It got so lonely here at the ranch with no one but Mom and an occasional work hand to talk to. The herders were always nice to her, but Mom never left her alone with them and they really didn't have anything in common with her. Maybe it wouldn't hurt to be a little bit nice to Shelley Ennison.

"Come on. I'll show you how to feed the lambs. But next time you visit, you should wear blue jeans and boots."

"I don't have any boots."

Anne shrugged. "Then just wear tennis shoes."

She led Shelley into the next pen. Shelley held the bucket of milk while Anne used a funnel to fill seven bottles. Shelley seemed eager to help and Anne appreciated the company and the help with her chores. But she sure wished Shelley's dad was a rancher instead of a ranger.

CHAPTER FOUR

"What happened?" Melanie ran across the gravel driveway toward the barn.

Anne and Shelley hobbled toward her. Shelley howled in pain, her bare legs streaming blood.

"Shelley! Are you okay?" Scott raced ahead, his face creased with concern.

"Shelley tripped and fell on a bale of barbed wire. It cut her legs up real bad." Anne had one of Shelley's arms draped across her shoulders as she helped the other girl limp to the house.

Without a word, Scott scooped Shelley into his strong arms, murmuring soothing words of comfort. Blood smeared his Forest Service shirt and name badge, but he couldn't care less.

Melanie moved into action, scurrying to the back door of the house. "I've got a first aid kit. Bring her inside."

Scott followed quickly and Anne held the

door open while he stepped into the utility room.

"Sit there on one of the kitchen chairs," Melanie called over her shoulder.

Scott stepped into the kitchen and sat cradling Shelley on his lap. The girl continued to sob while Melanie hurried into the bathroom, retrieved the hydrogen peroxide, salve and bandages, then returned and knelt beside the girl's injured legs.

Shelley buried her tear-streaked face against her father's chest. He rubbed her back, soothing her in low tones. Anne stood beside the door in her blue jeans and work boots, looking helpless.

Melanie smiled at the injured girl. "You'll be okay, sweetheart. We'll get this taken care of and you'll be good as new. Did you like the dogie lambs?"

Shelley gave an almost inaudible nod. "Y-yes."

"Did Anne show you how to feed them?"

"Uh-huh."

"Did they almost knock you off your feet with their exuberance?" Melanie kept up a steady stream of questions, trying to take Shelley's mind off her injuries. It helped some as the girl's tears faded to breathless hiccups.

While she cleansed the wounds, Melanie

couldn't help glancing up at Scott. She wasn't used to tender displays of affection from a man. She'd grown up at Opal Ranch with a kind but gruff father whom she'd only seen cry the day they buried her mother five years earlier. Dad had died shortly afterward, leaving her and Aaron to run the ranch alone.

Although he'd worked hard when he was sober, Aaron never offered her any comfort, not even when she went into labor with Anne. He hadn't cared for much except buying more booze. She sorely missed her mother's compassion and gentle faith.

The compassion on Scott's face surprised her. She never expected the new ranger to love a child the way Scott Ennison seemed to love his daughter. She'd been raised to think of rangers as less than human. Monsters that hated ranchers and ate little children for lunch.

Melanie almost laughed out loud at her wayward thoughts. This ranger seemed completely human, but Shelley might not want to stay here at Opal Ranch after having her legs torn up by barbed wire. "There, I think we've cleansed all the scratches and I put a pain-relieving salve and bandages on the bigger cuts. Do they still hurt?"

Shelley nodded while Scott wiped the

tears from her cheeks.

Melanie stood and squeezed Shelley's hand. "It'll feel better soon. I'm sorry you fell down, sweetie. Would some cookies and ice cream help you feel better?"

Shelley gave a wan smile as she slid off her father's lap. Without a word, Anne raced to the freezer and pulled out a container of vanilla ice cream, which she set on the counter.

While Melanie reached for the bowls and a scoop, Scott stepped near and whispered for her ears alone, "Thank you. It seems you're always there to save us."

Melanie pretended not to hear as she reached for the plate of cookies he'd brought her. She didn't want to be there for this man and his lovable daughter. For so long, she'd been strong on her own, fretting over her sheep, her child and the mortgage. Carrying the burdens of the ranch while Aaron slept off another night of drinking.

For several years, Melanie had longed to hand her burdens over to someone else and had come to rely on the Lord. She liked being single and making her own decisions without repercussions, but she wished she had the strength of a man to carry her through.

Now this handsome stranger had thrust

his way into her life. Within a few years, he'd be transferred someplace else. That's how it worked in the Forest Service. Rangers always moved on after a short time. Besides, she didn't want another man in her life. Ever. It hurt too much. And she had Anne to think about. She could have no future with Scott Ennison. No lasting ties. It'd be best not to let him get too close.

She inwardly groaned. Maybe she shouldn't have agreed to watch Shelley. But Scott's lonely little girl struck a chord in her, and she really did need his help around the ranch. For her own peace of mind, she resolved to keep this arrangement strictly business. She was Shelley's child care provider and Scott was her work hand. It had to stay that way. Period.

"I like Anne." Shelley leaned against Scott's side as he drove them home. She sat in the middle section of the seat, her seat belt across her stomach as she leaned on her left side to take the weight off the scratches and cuts on her right leg.

Holding tight to the steering wheel with his left hand, he snuggled her closer with his right. It'd been a long time since she'd let him hug her. He missed the days when she'd been little and climbed up into his lap for a hug just because. Now, he knew she felt vulnerable after being hurt by the barbed wire. Otherwise, she'd be sitting firmly on the other side of the truck. "I'm glad you like Anne. You'll be staying with the McAllisters during the day while I'm at work. You think you'll like that, too?"

"Yeah, me and Anne are both half dogies."

He lifted one brow. "Half dogies?"

He listened with amusement while she explained about the orphan lambs. "You know you're not an orphan. Your mom's still alive."

"But she doesn't want us. She cheated with Malcolm Henley." She spoke with disgust.

Her words hit him like a slap to the face and he inhaled sharply. She knew Allison had had an affair. He'd never said a word to her about it. He thought about all the months of trying to speak kindly about her mother, trying to keep the ugly truth from Shelley. His daughter had known all along. Allison didn't want her. Didn't want either one of them. Now that he realized she knew the truth, he couldn't bring himself to cover it with a lie. "I'm sorry, sweetheart. I have no control over your mother, but I'll make a promise to you."

She looked up at him and waited, her wide

blue eyes shining with tears. How he wished he could ease her pain and loneliness.

"I'll never leave you. Not ever." And he meant it. Only death could force him to leave his beautiful child.

"Thanks, Daddy." She wrapped one thin arm across his abdomen, her small head nestled against his chest. He blinked to clear his eyes as he stared out the windshield. A feeling of love overwhelmed him and he patted her arm. How he loved her. All he wanted to do was protect her. To make her happy.

He hoped his agreement with Melanie wasn't a giant mistake. He hoped it would be good. For all of them.

The next morning, Scott pulled his blue truck into Melanie's front yard at exactly seven-thirty. He'd have just enough time to get Shelley settled and drive back into town to work. He'd made sure he drove his own truck to Opal Ranch. If he used a government truck for personal errands and someone complained, he could be fired. He didn't want to do anything to cause more trouble.

In spite of her sore legs, Shelley unsnapped her seat belt and hopped out. She beat Scott to the front porch where she stood on tiptoe to reach the horseshoe knocker on the front door. She tapped it twice.

At this cooler elevation, Scott wore long-sleeved shirts. Today, he felt exceptionally warm in his ranger uniform. As he sauntered past the front gate, he caught the cooling mist of water from the sprinkler on the lawn.

"You're not excited to be staying here, are you?" He couldn't help teasing Shelley, relieved to see her so happy for a change.

"Of course I am, silly! Anne says I can help her feed the lambs again. I like it here."

Good! He chuckled, not wanting to remind her that after the repetition of feeding lambs several times each day, she might not like the chore so much in a week. Ultimately, he knew this experience would be good for her. She'd have chores and a new friend to keep her busy. Finally, something was going right for them.

The door jerked open and Anne stood before them in blue jeans and bare feet.

"Hi." Shelley stepped inside without an invitation.

"Hi." Anne ignored Scott and moved back as he stood in the doorway.

Anne eyed Shelley's red-and-white tennis shoes and blue jeans before nodding her head in approval. "That's much better. Your pants will protect your legs from now on."

Shelley's smile widened.

As Scott stepped into the living room, he caught the scent of fresh-baked bread. He breathed in deeply, relishing the tantalizing aroma. It reminded him of home when he'd been a kid. Mom had baked bread almost every day when he was growing up. He couldn't remember a single time Allison made something from scratch. She preferred takeout.

He wiped his feet on the rag rug by the door. The tan carpets looked worn, but clean. A sofa and two recliners surrounded a large, glass-topped coffee table with a vase of field flowers in the center. Family pictures in gold frames lined the mantel of the fireplace. The large console TV set looked like it could serve as a boat anchor. It sat next to a bookcase filled with a variety of history books and old encyclopedias. In one corner of the room sat a small desk with a computer and a user's manual open on top of the keyboard. Everything looked tidy except for a stack of scrapbooks and photo albums piled on a card table. It looked like Melanie was working on some family projects.

"Hi there! Have you had breakfast?" Melanie bustled into the room, her cheeks flushed as she whipped her thick hair behind her head and tied it into a long ponytail with a blue scrunchie.

The aroma of her homemade bread called to him, but he nodded his head and wished he didn't have to get to work so soon. He'd love to linger and chat, but he didn't have time. "Yeah, we've eaten." He inclined his chin toward the computer. "You learning how to use that machine?"

She grimaced, her button nose scrunching. "Yes, I'm sorry to say. It's a nightmare. I thought I should come in out of the dark ages and have a computer in the house for Anne. I thought it might make my payroll easier, but the growing pains are causing me some angst. I've enrolled in a computer basics class at the civic center in town and I'm determined to figure it out."

He chuckled, enjoying the fact that she was so determined to learn something new. The more he discovered about this woman, the more he liked her. "Maybe I can help. I'm pretty good with computers."

Her eyes widened and he saw a glimmer of desperation there before a barrier dropped over her face, as if she remembered who he was. "Maybe. Don't worry about Shelley. We've got lots of chores to do today and I'm looking forward to the girls helping." Melanie rested her hand on Shelley's shoulder and gave the girl a warm smile.

"That sounds great. I know Shelley's excited to be with Anne. Do you like to go riding?" He smiled at Anne, but the girl quirked her mouth in disgust and turned away.

Scott took the snub hard. He didn't know why this girl's approval mattered so much to him, but he wished she'd give him a chance.

"Come on, I'll get my boots on and we can get to work." Anne tugged on Shelley's arm, pulling her toward the kitchen.

Shelley paused, wrapping her arms around Scott for a quick hug. "See you later, Daddy."

"Okay, munchkin. Have a good day." He gave her a peck on the forehead before the girl hurried after Anne. Though he could no longer see them, he heard their happy chatter as they discussed the baby lambs. Relief flood him. He hadn't felt settled and confident about his daughter's well-being for almost six months. It felt good to know she was happy and safe, and he had Melanie to thank for that.

"We'll see you later this afternoon." Melanie hovered beside the door, a veiled invitation for him to leave.

"Before I go, I wanted to give you this." He handed her a yellow flyer.

"What's this?" Her gaze scanned the page.

"I'm planning to post these around town. I'm holding a special meeting in two weeks with the local ranchers to discuss grievances and possible solutions. I thought you'd like to attend."

"Yes, I have a few grievances of my own."

He quirked a brow. "Such as?"

"The coyote problem has been exceptionally bad this year. A number of us ranchers complained about it to the previous ranger, but nothing ever got done."

He nodded. "Okay, I'll see what I can do. Anything else?"

"I'd sure feel better if we could do something about the larkspur covering part of the mountain pastures over by Gaylin Canyon. The noxious plants are killing my sheep."

"I have a crew of workers that can go in and spray and dig it out. I can have it done by end of the week."

She didn't say anything, but her forehead crinkled with skepticism. He could tell that she didn't believe he'd do anything; it delighted him to prove her wrong.

He turned to leave, but she stopped him, her lips pursed together. "Scott, it's wonderful that you're making an effort to talk to the ranchers and I don't want to discourage you, but don't be surprised if your meeting doesn't go too well."

What did she mean? "You don't think many ranchers will attend?"

"Oh, yes. You'll have a packed house . . . filled with very angry people."

"That bad, huh?"

She took a deep breath and let it go. "I'm afraid so. I just want to caution you."

Interesting. She didn't trust him or really even like him, yet she thought enough to warn him. "What do you think I should do?"

She licked her bottom lip, thinking this over. Ah, he'd turned the tables on her, asking her advice.

"Just speak calmly no matter how much they bait you and be patient if some of the ranchers start out on the attack. And keep your promises to them. Every. Single. One." A stern glint shimmered in her eyes. She meant what she said.

He nodded. "Counsel taken. Don't worry. I've handled an angry crowd before. I'm a good listener and I know what I can and can't do. We'll reach some agreements and get along just fine."

As he stepped to the door, he heard her

whisper behind him. "I hope so. I really do."

He hoped so, too.

CHAPTER FIVE

After lunch, Melanie tossed another load of laundry into the washing machine, then stepped out on the back porch and rang the bell hanging from the eaves. It kept her from straining her vocal cords when she or Anne needed to find each other around the ranch.

Anne and Shelley came running from the lambing sheds, Bob close on their heels. The old dog was one of the best sheepdogs Melanie had ever seen. He just couldn't do the work anymore, so she kept him here at the ranch instead of up on the mountain with a herder.

Melanie hid a smile. She didn't really need to ring the bell, because she knew where the girls were. They'd spent the morning rushing through their chores so they could spend more time with the dogie lambs.

They arrived at the back door, out of breath, their faces glowing with joy. Melanie reached out and smoothed the collar of

Shelley's shirt into place. "You girls think you can leave those lambs long enough to make a trip into town with me? We need some supplies and I thought we'd stop at the drive-in for ice cream cones."

"Yeah!" Anne crowed.

"For sure," Shelley agreed.

"Let's go, then." Carrying her purse, Melanie headed to the truck with the girls racing ahead. Rather than letting the arthritic dog jump up, Anne lifted Bob into the back, then closed the tailgate.

"Snap on your seat belts," Melanie said as she tossed her purse onto the front seat and inserted the key into the ignition.

The girls obeyed and Anne flipped on the radio. They listened to a country-western song as they drove down the dirt lane leading to the main road. The girls sang along, their voices high and sweet. Melanie smiled, wishing it could always be like this. She feared the newness would wear off and the girls might start fighting, as most children did. She hoped they remained good friends. She didn't want to tell Scott that he'd have to find another child care provider for Shelley. For some crazy reason, she wanted this arrangement to work.

In town, she drove down Main Street and headed to Wiley's Feed and Grain. She parked out front and the girls hopped out and followed her into the store, but Bob remained in the truck, panting. Inside, the air smelled of alfalfa and leather. Melanie's booted heels clicked against the rough wood floors.

"How are the McAllisters today?" Carl Wiley greeted them, his whiskered chops plumped in a big smile. "And who's your new friend?" He held out a tub of wrapped lollipops and let each girl take one.

"Thank you." Shelley returned his warm smile, reaching to stroke a gray cat that lay sprawled in a shady spot on the front counter.

"This is Shelley," Anne said. "She's staying with us while her dad works."

Carl's bushy eyebrows drew together as he set the tub aside and crossed his arms over his gray plaid shirt. "And who's your father?"

"Scott Ennison," Shelley responded in a shy tone, her attention focused on her lollipop and the cat. In her innocence, she missed the dark scowl that covered Carl's bearded face.

Melanie saw it and brushed past, hoping to bypass any censure. After the numerous times she'd come into town to fetch Aaron after he'd been brawling or passed out in a

90

drunken stupor, she'd become inured to people's disapproval. This time, her efforts were wasted. Carl followed her over to the salt licks stacked on the floor.

"You're tending the ranger's kid?" he whispered rather harshly.

"That's right. She's a good friend for Anne to play with. Is there a law against it or something?" She jerked on her leather work gloves.

"No, of course not, but I never would have thought you'd let the ranger's kid play with Anne. Not after what happened to —"

"I'll need two salt licks. Can you put them in my truck?" She cut him off on purpose, wishing she could forget that terrible night when Aaron died.

Carl was right, of course. After everything Ben Stimpson had put her and Aaron through, she still couldn't believe she'd agreed to watch Shelley. And yet, in her heart, she knew it was the right thing to do.

"Sure." Carl picked up the salt licks and carried them up front, then rounded the counter. "You're playing with fire, Mrs. McAllister. After losing Aaron, I would've thought you of all people would have better sense than to —"

She met his eyes and cut him off again. "I also need two hundred pounds of texturized lamb starter. I like that stuff with cracked and rolled grains and liquid molasses. I also need some vaccinations for clostridial disease."

"You got some sheep with the bloat?"

"A few. Can you load everything in the truck for me?"

He pursed his lips, but turned to go outside and fill her order, muttering as he went. "Makes no never mind to me, but when folks hear about this, they won't like it."

His voice faded. Melanie released a long sigh and looked up at the ceiling. She didn't care if people approved of her. When she'd agreed to watch Shelley, she figured people in town would hear about it sooner or later, but she didn't think she'd have to deal with it quite this soon. She couldn't very well back out now. Scott needed her help. Besides, she wasn't about to let public opinion dictate what she did or didn't do. It wasn't anyone's business who came into her home.

When Carl returned, she paid her bill with cash, called to the girls and walked out, thinking that was the end of the matter. She'd forgotten how quickly gossip traveled in this small town.

After they arrived at the general store, she shut off the truck and stared at the front window of Donaldson's General Store, unable to believe her eyes. Her fingers tightened around the steering wheel. A hot-pink sign with big black lettering read: No Service to Forest Rangers.

This just kept getting better and better.

As she got out of the truck, Melanie hoped Shelley wouldn't notice. She tried to tell herself it didn't matter to her, but she couldn't help feeling protective of the little girl and her father. Why? Why did she care about Shelley and Scott Ennison and how the townsfolk treated them?

"Mom, what — ?" Anne hesitated in front of the door, reading the sign.

"Never mind. Let's just get our shopping done."

"What does it mean?" Shelley asked.

Anne shrugged. "They don't like your dad."

"Anne." Melanie spoke in a disapproving tone.

"Well, it's true," Anne said.

"Why not? What did he do to them?" Shelley asked in a hurt voice.

Anne gave an impatient huff. "I already explained this to you yesterday, remember? Your dad's a ranger and most everyone else is a rancher. Rangers and ranchers don't get along."

"Anne, that's not true," Melanie gently chided. "We're ranchers and we get along just fine with Scott."

Anne sneered, but kept her silence.

"I still don't see why we can't all get along and be friends," Shelley said plaintively.

From the mouths of babes.

Melanie was trying so hard to get along with the new ranger, but she had doubts. She just hoped he didn't let all the ranchers down.

She briefly considered having the girls wait outside in the truck. The Donaldsons were hardened ranchers who'd had several run-ins with the previous ranger. While Nina Donaldson ran the grocery store, her husband, Frank, and their three sons managed Donaldson Cattle Ranch. They had money and tended to think they owned the rest of the town, too.

Not her. Although Frank Donaldson's property bordered her own and he'd asked repeatedly for her to sell her ranch to him, Melanie refused to let him intimidate her. She always paid her grocery bill in cash, determined not to be beholden to them.

Something went cold inside Melanie. Why should Shelley be punished for her father's profession? And for that matter, Melanie had seen every indication that Scott planned

94

to work amicably with the ranchers in Snyderville. He hadn't done anything to hurt them. Of course, he hadn't done anything yet to win their trust, either. But he seemed so determined to do the right thing. Maybe he wasn't like the other rangers. Maybe he would make a difference.

Maybe.

As she urged the girls inside, she made a decision right then and there. For good or bad, she'd agreed to watch Scott's daughter, which meant she would protect the little girl. And she intended to do just that. Scott would have to handle the rest of his problems on his own, but she would not allow anyone to harangue or injure Shelley while the little girl was in her care.

Somehow making this inward commitment gave Melanie the courage to follow through with her plans. As expected on a Tuesday afternoon, the store had several people pushing shopping carts down the narrow aisles. Taking out her grocery list and a pen, Melanie barely spared the front cash register a glance as she headed for the canned goods.

"Afternoon, Melanie." Nina Donaldson, a tall, large-boned woman with a long, hawkish nose, called to her. Dressed in blue jeans and wearing a long white apron, Nina stood beside a rack of magazines and holding a broom in her hands.

"Good afternoon, Nina. How's that cold you were fighting?"

"Fine, I'm over it now."

"Good." Melanie jerked her thumb toward the front window. "What's with the sign?"

Nina waved her hand. "Oh, that. We're just hoping to let the new ranger know where he stands with us."

"You don't think that's a bit childish?"

Nina's mouth dropped open and Melanie instantly regretted baiting the woman.

"Maybe you should give him a chance, first," Melanie hurried on.

"He's a ranger," Nina said, as if that settled it. "Have you met him yet?"

"Yes, and I found him quite amenable. I think he really wants to help us ranchers and I plan to give him a chance." Melanie took Shelley's hand and picked out a shopping cart, turning her back on any further comments from Nina. She pushed the cart to the back of the store, fuming with anger. Melanie had been on the receiving end of Nina's sharp tongue often enough when Aaron was alive and she felt sympathy for Scott. He was a human being, even if he was a ranger. He needed to buy groceries and eat, just like everyone else.

Again, she tried to tell herself this wasn't her problem and she should stay out of it. What did she care if the Donaldsons refused to sell Scott any groceries? She couldn't help wondering if she'd be so quick to defend him if he wasn't so handsome and charming.

Shelley's small fingers curled around Melanie's hand, so innocent and trusting. "Melanie, what did that sign mean?"

This was one reason she cared. When adults acted up, the children often bore the brunt of their stupidity. Shelley's voice vibrated with emotion, exposing her vulnerability. She didn't deserve this treatment.

Trying not to overreact, Melanie reached for three gallons of milk. It wasn't surprising that Shelley had read the sign. Both girls were young, but they weren't stupid. "Just ignore it, sweetie. It's not your concern."

"But it said no service to forest rangers and my dad is a ranger."

"Your dad will deal with it," Anne said

"But does that mean they won't let Dad buy groceries anymore?"

Melanie reached for a block of unsalted butter. "I'm not sure. He'll have to talk to them, but don't worry. Your dad will take good care of you."

Shelley didn't look convinced. "Will they

let you buy your groceries if I'm with you?"

"Yeah, Mom," Anne piped in. "What if we can't buy food, either?"

Melanie sighed in frustration. "You're both worrying for nothing. We'll all be fine. Let's just finish buying our groceries and go get our ice cream, okay? We don't want this to ruin our day. We can talk more about it in the truck when we're alone."

Thankfully, the girls didn't say another word as Melanie completed her shopping and wheeled her cart up front to the check-out counter.

As if understanding the volatile situation they were in, Shelley gestured to Anne. "I'm gonna wait outside."

When Anne followed Shelley out the door, Melanie breathed a sigh of relief. What a coward she was. She'd be in a world of hurt if she had to drive all the way to Evanston to obtain supplies, but it looked like Scott would have to do just that. How unfair. And cruel.

"Who's Anne's new friend?" Nina asked as she began ringing up Melanie's purchases.

"Her name's Shelley." She decided that less information might be better at this point.

"Is she a relative?"

Melanie could see Nina trying to act indifferent, but the woman's eagle eyes glanced over to the front door and then back to Melanie's face. The two girls stood just outside in the shade. They weren't speaking and Melanie wondered if Shelley knew how much Anne resented Scott. Against Melanie's wishes, Aaron had poisoned Anne's head with all kinds of nonsense about evil rangers. If not for that barrier, the two girls could be best friends.

"No, just a friend staying with us for a time." Okay, she'd told no lies. It worked.

Before Nina could ask more questions, Melanie counted out the money and slapped it down on the counter. "Thanks, Nina. See you next week."

Trying not to move with a sense of urgency, Melanie wheeled her cart outside to her truck, stashed the plastic bags in back with Bob, then hopped inside with the girls and drove away. Nina stood at the dingy front window, watching them go. And Melanie knew without a doubt that by closing time, Nina would try to find out who Shelley was, which meant she'd discover that the girl's father was the ranger. When Melanie returned to shop on Saturday, she could very well find a sign posted on the window that read: No Service to the Mc-

Allisters.

Melanie's stomach tightened painfully. What had she gotten herself into?

"You okay, Mom?" Anne's eyes crinkled with concern.

Melanie patted the girl on the knee. "Yes, sweetheart, I'm fine. I guess I'm just not very tolerant of bigots."

"What's a big idiot?" Shelley asked.

Melanie laughed. "It's pronounced bi-got. And it's someone who is intolerant of other people simply because of their profession."

"Is that why the store doesn't want to sell my dad groceries? Because they're a bigot?"

"I'm afraid so, and it means the same as a big idiot, so you can say it either way."

"But why don't they like Daddy? He's an awfully nice man."

"You and I know that, but they think he's bad, just like the previous ranger who used to live here."

"Oh." Confusion replaced the hurt in Shelley's eyes. She didn't understand. Neither did Melanie. And she didn't want to try and explain it, either.

"I'll tell you what. I'll talk to your father about it when he comes to pick you up in a couple of hours and then you can ask him all the questions you want. But right now, let's forget about it and go get our ice cream cones. Okay?"

"Okay." Shelley nodded, but her smile didn't quite reach her eyes.

They all ate their ice cream in silence as Melanie drove them home. By the time they returned to Opal Ranch and put the groceries away, their fun afternoon had dissipated into disappointment. Even the lambs couldn't make Shelley smile. The girl watched the clock, biting her fingernails, waiting for Scott to pick her up.

While she mucked out a corral, Melanie tried to forget the glare of that pink sign blazing across her memory. Tried to forget the deep hurt in Shelley's eyes. After all, this wasn't Melanie's problem. Scott was a strong man and he'd deal with the Donaldsons. She didn't care where he went to buy his groceries. It didn't matter to her at all.

Yeah, and sheep could fly.

"Daddy!" Shelley burst through the screen door and ran down the front porch as he walked past the hollyhocks to Melanie's house.

"Oof!" Scott absorbed the tight hug from his daughter, caught off guard. What had gotten into her? He couldn't remember the last time she had hugged him this often. Staying at the McAllisters' house was definitely good for her. "Hey, munchkin. Did you have a good day?"

"Kinda, but then we went into town and there was a sign at the grocery store."

She told him all about it as he walked with her to the house. He listened intently, feeling a flush of anger prickle his skin. The Donaldsons refused to sell him any groceries. He couldn't believe it.

"Why don't they like us, Dad?"

What could he say when he didn't know the answer? "I don't know, honey. I think they're afraid of me."

"But why? You wouldn't hurt them."

Her faith in him touched his heart. "No, I wouldn't do anything to purposefully hurt them."

Melanie greeted them at the door, concern filling her eyes. As she indicated a chair in the living room, he waved at Anne, who frowned and quickly slipped out the back door. He sat down, listening while Shelley poured out the story. Melanie didn't say a word, just stood leaning against the bookcase, her gaze pinned on Shelley's animated face.

"We'll starve if they don't let us buy groceries, Dad. What will we eat?" Shelley's voice rose to a shrill tone. This had frightened her and he didn't like it at all.

Scott reached out and cupped her cheek, looking directly into her eyes. "Honey, I know I'm not much of a cook, but have I ever let you go hungry — even once?"

She shook her head. A fat tear rolled down her cheek and he wiped it away with his thumb.

"And will you trust me when I tell you that we'll always have plenty of food to eat in our house?"

"You promise?"

"I promise."

She gave a hesitant nod. He was conscious of Anne standing in the doorway to the kitchen, her arms folded as she listened intently.

More than anything, he wanted his child to believe in him. And it occurred to him then that he wasn't just fighting for the confidence of the local ranchers. He was also fighting for the trust of his daughter.

No matter what happened from this point on, he resolved to be strong for both of them. "And will you trust me if I tell you that everything's gonna be okay and I won't let anything bad happen to us?"

Another nod and tremulous smile. "Yes, Daddy. I trust you."

So maybe that rotten sign at the grocery store had been worth it, just to bring out

Shelley's loyalty and trust. "Okay, then. Why don't you wait for me by the truck and I'll be right out after I've had a moment to talk to Melanie."

Wiping her eyes, Shelley smiled and trotted outside with Anne. Scott watched the girls go, seriously contemplating his options. He fought off the temptation to drive directly to the Sheriff's Office and demand that the single law enforcement officer in this region put a stop to this nonsense. But what good would filing a complaint do? Obviously, the Donaldsons wanted a fight and he wasn't about to give it to them.

"You saw the sign?" he asked Melanie.

"Yes, it was there."

He stood up to go, mentally making a list of the cans and boxes of food in his pantry at home. "I think we can make it until Saturday and then I'll have to make a trip into Evanston."

"And?" Melanie said.

"And what?"

"You're not going to do anything about it?"

"Like what?"

"It's illegal, Scott. They can't do this."

"I know, but a big fight is the last thing I need right now. I'll have to shop in Evanston for the time being. But if I show up on

104

your doorstep asking for a cup of sugar or a glass of milk, you'll understand why."

"You can't drive into Evanston every time you need a cube of butter."

He shrugged. "We'll have to do without a few things now and then, but we'll get by. I've faced worse situations in my life." Including times when his father had drunk up all the money so they couldn't buy groceries at all. He'd helped his mother grow large gardens, shucking corn and shelling peas, which she canned and put in the pantry. He'd learned to hide a few dollars when he had it, so they could buy milk. He couldn't remember a time when he didn't have a part-time job after school to help support the family.

"And what about other times?" Melanie asked.

"What do you mean?"

She stepped closer and looked up at him, her intense gaze holding him captive. He caught her scent, a combination of baked bread and fruity shampoo. He couldn't decide which he liked best.

"What about when Shelley starts school in the fall? Are you prepared for the other children to tease her and the teachers to treat her a bit roughly?"

He clenched his hands. "Anyone who

treats my little girl badly will have to answer to me."

And he meant it. He could handle whatever anyone threw at him, but he would never tolerate anyone picking on Shelley simply because of his job.

"Do you have a problem watching her?" he asked.

She must have caught the brusque anger in his voice, because she visibly flinched. He didn't mean to frighten her, but right now he was furious. If she wanted to back out on their deal, he needed to know. Could he trust her to treat Shelley with kindness? Just how deep did her resentment toward Ben Stimpson go?

"Of course not, Scott," she reassured him. "Before we drove into town, the girls were happy. They work and play well together and get along just fine, except for —" She bit her bottom lip.

"Except for me."

She nodded. "Shelley's a sweet girl, Scott. I agreed to watch her as long as the two girls got along well and I meant it. I see no need for Shelley to leave. And you can rest assured that I'll treat her well while she's in my care."

"I'm very aware that Anne doesn't like me. Why doesn't she dislike Shelley, too?"

She scrunched one shoulder up to her ear. "I can't explain it, but Anne seems to have taken Shelley under her wing. Last night she told me they are kindred spirits because they're both half dogies."

His mouth twitched. "Shelley mentioned something about that."

"Yeah . . . because both girls are missing one of their parents, they've decided that makes them half dogies."

He smiled; he couldn't help it. "Doesn't that beat all? It'd be funny if it weren't so sad."

"I know. I wish more than anything that I could give Anne a loving father."

"I feel the same way about Shelley. I tried everything I could think of to make my marriage with Allison work, but she came to hate me for the very same reason Anne doesn't like me. Because I'm a ranger."

And then he asked the question that had been haunting him since he met this woman up on the lonely mountain. "Do you hate me, too?"

"Of course not. Don't be silly." She didn't hesitate, which he took for honesty.

Relief flooded Scott's heart and he couldn't explain why it meant so much to him that Melanie liked him. He knew he liked her, but that was as far as he was prepared to take their relationship. He had to put Shelley's needs first and already they were in a difficult predicament.

"I don't hate anyone, although I do hate certain things," she said.

"Such as?"

"Alcohol."

He held her gaze. "We have that in common."

"I won't tolerate the stuff in my house ever again. I loved my husband, but I don't miss his drinking. Not after all the pain he caused us in the past with —"

She didn't finish her statement, as if realizing she had confided too much. Scott understood the passionate tone of her voice. He remembered feeling much the same way; he'd missed his father after he'd died and yet Scott had been relieved that Dad was gone, too. Life had been difficult after Dad's death, but at least they didn't have to fear being woken up in the middle of the night to a harsh beating. It didn't make sense, loving and hating someone simultaneously. He figured anyone who'd lived with an alcoholic would understand.

"I know what you mean," he said. "My father was an alcoholic when he died. It caused enough sadness in my life when I was young that it cured me of drinking, even socially."

Her eyes widened with surprise. "I didn't know. Our girls *do* have a lot in common. If not for the Lord, I don't know how I'd still be hanging on."

He found it difficult not to snort with disgust. Instead, he looked away, hoping to hide his skeptical expression. She caught his cynicism anyway.

"You don't believe in God?" she asked.

"Yeah, but the Lord and I don't have much time for each other."

"What do you mean?"

"Let's just say we leave each other alone."

A tolerant smile softened her face. "You sound rather cynical. God never abandons any of us. He's just a prayer away. It's usually us who pull away from Him."

What could Scott say to that without offending her? He decided to play it safe and bit his tongue, breathing a sigh of relief when she didn't push the issue.

"Our girls have become fast friends. I don't want to let what happened in town ruin that for them."

He agreed. "I'm hoping to show Anne that I'm not the ogre she thinks I am."

He tensed, awaiting her reaction. Except for Jim and Karen, Melanie had become his only ally in Snyderville and he hated to lose their tentative friendship. What if Melanie got scared off by the censure from the other ranchers? He didn't know what he'd do if she refused to provide child care for Shelley.

"Don't worry, Scott. I can handle this. I was just caught off guard. I'll restructure my schedule so I can protect Shelley better on shopping day. Nina never works on Saturdays, so I'll do my shopping then."

Her loyalty touched him deeply. He couldn't help resenting Allison for not being here to help protect their daughter. Melanie had shown more generosity toward Shelley than the girl's own mother.

If he were honest, he would confess that he expected Melanie to break their business deal. After all, his problems weren't her problems. She had her hands full running her ranch. Seeing the kindly light in her eyes and hearing her words of comfort reassured him as nothing else could. Both he and Shelley needed the McAllisters right now. Badly.

"Thanks, Mel. I appreciate it more than I can say."

She walked him to the door. As she waved goodbye, he looked over and saw Anne sitting on the porch swing watching him. He could count on Melanie, but he wasn't so sure about Anne. The girl seemed to genuinely like Shelley. It was him she disliked so vehemently. And he had no doubt Melanie would put Anne first. If he became too big a problem, Melanie would need to curtail their tentative friendship. Scott couldn't blame her. He'd do the same thing for Shelley. He just hoped it didn't come to that.

When he'd accepted this job assignment, he hadn't realized how difficult things might get. He didn't like being a pariah in town. If only he could prove everyone wrong. If only he could show them that he was a friend, not a foe.

He'd get his chance soon enough, at the ranchers' meeting he'd scheduled. From what Melanie had told him, every rancher would be there. If he was a praying man, he'd ask God for help. But he hadn't prayed since the week before Allison left him, and he didn't want to start now.

CHAPTER SIX

On Friday evening, Scott arrived to pick up Shelley and stayed to work for a couple of hours. He wore a plain cotton shirt that matched the crystal blue of his eyes. Melanie exhaled slowly, grateful he'd changed out of his ranger uniform. She chuckled when she imagined what Frank and Nina Donaldson would say if they saw him out in her hay fields moving sprinkler pipe.

"You sure you know what to do?" she asked as he braced one hand on the top rail and hopped the fence with ease.

"Yep." He didn't comment further as he reached back for Shelley to assist her as she straddled the fence. When he reached to help Anne, the little girl backed away, her eyes narrowed. Scott didn't push the issue. He dropped his hand to his side, then turned and walked toward the main water valve.

Melanie had turned off the water an hour

earlier so the pipes would drain and be less cumbersome to move. She stood leaning against the splintered fence, shading her eyes from the afternoon sunshine. Staring after him as he ambled away, she couldn't help but admire his muscular physique. He seemed self-assured on a ranch, but did he really know what to do? Uncertainty filled Melanie for a few moments until he unhooked the outlet, then headed for the little gas-driven engine. After turning it on, he started moving each giant wheel sprinkler into a nice, straight line. Yep, he knew what he was doing. She'd check back later to make sure that he rehooked the flexible pipe and turned the water back on.

Shelley trotted after her father, but Anne stayed behind with Melanie.

"You don't want to help move the sprinklers?" Melanie asked as she walked to the barn.

Anne pursed her lips together and shook her head.

"You know, you're not being very fair to Scott," she observed.

"I don't know why you're nice to him. Dad wouldn't like it." Without letting her mom respond, Anne raced out of the barn and ran into the house.

This was getting out of hand.

Melanie threw hay to the horses, finished filling the water trough, then headed to the house. Inside the back porch, she pulled off her boots before walking in her stocking feet to Anne's bedroom. The door was closed and she rapped softly with her knuckles.

No answer.

She opened the door just a bit and peeked in. Her daughter sat on her bed glaring across the room.

"Go away!" Anne whirled about and lay down, burying her face against a pillow.

"Sweetheart, we need to talk." The bed bounced softly as Melanie sat on the edge and reached out to caress Anne's back. The girl jerked away, yanking the pillow over the top of her head.

This wasn't going to be easy.

"Anne, I didn't realize you felt so strongly about this."

"Well, I do." Anne's voice sounded muffled and filled with emotion.

"I'm sorry. I should have talked to you before I agreed to watch Shelley. If you don't want the Ennisons here, I'll send them away. We'll get by somehow."

Anne rolled over and the pillow lowered just enough for Melanie to see her daughter's big, tear-filled eyes. "You'd do that for me?"

temper and a penchant for booze. The saddest part of all was that Aaron was such a good, hardworking man when he wasn't drinking. He could have been so much more, if only he hadn't been addicted to alcohol.

"Scott isn't your father, Anne. Why don't you just enjoy having Shelley here and leave everything else to me?" Melanie wanted to point out that Scott didn't drink, but she didn't want to hurt Anne with the reminder.

"All right, Shelley can stay."

"And Scott? You can't have Shelley without her dad. Remember that she loves her father as much as you loved yours. Without him, Shelley would be all alone in the world."

A light clicked on inside Anne's eyes as this fully dawned on her. "You're right, Shelley needs us real bad. Right now, she's just a half dogie. Without her dad, she'd be a complete dogie."

If it weren't so bittersweet, Melanie would have laughed. She knew this was very serious to Anne and Shelley. Somehow the two girls were able to relate to each other because they'd both lost a parent recently. "That's right. She loves her dad, too."

"Poor Shelley. It's so sad that her dad's a ranger."

She shook her head. "Sweetheart, Scott is a good man. I've seen it in him. You're not being fair."

"But Dad said that forest rangers are dirty rotten, no good —"

Melanie held up a hand, fearing that her daughter might utter some of the foul language she'd heard Aaron use. "That's enough. I know what your dad said and he was wrong. I won't have that kind of language in our home anymore."

The girl's mouth dropped open and her eyes rounded with shock.

Melanie looked her daughter right in the eye. "How would you feel if Shelley believed that all ranchers were horrible and called your daddy bad names?"

"But we're not. Well, maybe Mr. Donaldson is rotten. He was never nice to Daddy, but that's different."

"How?"

"That's just the way Mr. Donaldson is. But Arnie Pike is a nice rancher. He helped us sometimes when Dad was sick."

Sick. What a simple word to describe Aaron's drunken stupors. It still hadn't dawned on Anne that, during those times, Melanie took her daughter up on the mountain to shield her from her father's foul temper. Melanie had borne the brunt of it instead. Anne was young enough to still idolize her father. And Melanie wasn't about to change that perception. At least not until Anne was older, so she could understand that her daddy also had some very good qualities.

When he wasn't drinking.

"So it wouldn't be fair to say that *all* ranchers are rotten, right?" she said, hoping she'd gotten her point across.

"Maybe, but I still don't like Shelley's dad. He's nothing more than a fancy-talking bureaucrat."

That was Aaron talking again. How many times had Melanie heard her husband say the very same thing? How she wished Aaron had been more careful what he'd said around their impressionable daughter. Now Melanie had her hands full trying to deal with Anne's biased opinions. "Remember I said no more name calling?"

Anne frowned.

"Scott has spoken pretty plainly to us so far. He hasn't used much fancy talk."

"But he hasn't kept his promises to us, either."

"He'll need more time for that, but he's out working in our fields right now. He's kept that promise."

Anne sat up. "We'll see. The proof is in

the pudding."

Now the girl was repeating what Melanie often said. Kids were so easily influenced by what they saw and heard from their parents.

"That's fair enough. We all prove ourselves by our words and deeds. But in the meantime, you need to be polite to Scott."

Anne huffed out a breath. "If you say so . . . but I don't have to be his friend, do I?"

"If he asks you a question, you should politely respond, but no, you don't have to be friends. Okay?" That concession wouldn't hurt after all.

"Okay."

Melanie hugged her daughter tight, overwhelmed by love and gratitude. God had taken so much from them, but He had given them so much, too. "I love you, sweetheart. You're my whole world."

"I love you, too, Mom, but you're squashing my eye."

Melanie laughed and let her daughter go. "Why don't you go out and say goodbye to Shelley. I think she and her dad should be about ready to leave and you don't want her to think you don't like her anymore."

"Is he gonna be here on Saturday?" Her voice sounded hopeful to see Shelley, yet guarded at the same time.

"Yes, we need to make a camp run in the afternoon to take supplies to Alfonso up on the mountain. Scott has agreed to help us do that."

"He just wants to spy on us." Anne's forehead crinkled in a scowl.

"No. He wants to see how he can help us. In return for me watching Shelley, he'll work here at the ranch. Remember, we just talked about this?" To make her point, Melanie allowed a twinge of sternness to enter her voice. As a loving mother, it was her responsibility to cultivate good manners in her daughter.

"Yeah, yeah. I got it." Anne didn't look convinced.

Okay, baby steps here. It would take time to change Anne's mind. Melanie hoped and prayed that Scott didn't let them down. She didn't dare admit that her daughter had voiced some of her own concerns. What if Scott didn't keep his promises to them? What if he was all talk and no show like the last ranger? They were in a vulnerable position right now and Scott had the power to push them out of business. Opal Ranch had been in Melanie's family for four generations. She didn't know where they would go or what she would do if they lost their home.

Doubt speared Melanie's heart. If bad

weather, coyotes, grizzlies and noxious plants killed many more sheep, they'd be in big trouble.

Please, Lord. Please help Scott keep his promises. Please help us keep the ranch.

The next Saturday morning, Scott and Shelley arrived at Opal Ranch at precisely eight o'clock. Insisting that they'd already eaten, Scott left Shelley in the house with Anne while he strode outside to work on the dilapidated toolshed.

As she stood at the kitchen sink washing dishes, Melanie watched him go, hardly able to take her eyes off him. Scott looked so different without his green Forest Service uniform. Today he'd dressed in faded blue jeans that accentuated his long legs, a navy blue T-shirt that molded his muscular arms and chest, and scuffed cowboy boots. The ranchers had called the last ranger Overbellie because his gut hung over his belt buckle, but that was not a word Melanie would have used to describe Scott. He looked real good. Too good.

Shaking her head, she focused on the sudsy water, wondering about the odd fluttering in her abdomen. She was a full-grown woman with a child of her own. She didn't have time to daydream about the handsome new ranger; a man her daughter could barely stand. He was Shelley's father and a work hand, nothing more.

An hour later, Melanie drove into town to pick up supplies for her sheep herder. Because she didn't want the girls upset by the sign on Donaldson's store, she left them home with Scott. He'd agreed to keep an eye on them, knowing the kids would spend every spare minute feeding the dogie lambs.

The truck bounced along the dirt road and it felt good to have a few minutes to herself. Even when Aaron had been alive, she'd rarely left Anne alone with him. He might start drinking and Melanie didn't want her little girl exposed to any possible abuse.

She rubbed her left arm almost subconsciously, remembering the night Aaron died as if it was yesterday. They'd had a horrible disagreement over him going out alone to move their sheep during the thunderstorm and he'd grabbed her, bruising her arm. No matter how much she had tried to quiet him, his yells had awakened Anne. The girl had screamed, asking her daddy not to leave. Begging him to take her with him. And later, when they found that he had died, Anne had blamed Melanie for not being able to keep him home.

Shaking off the horrible memory, Melanie blinked her eyes, realizing that she was crying. Even now that he was gone, Aaron's memory still haunted her. The rank stench of alcohol, the fights, the doubt and guilt. To lighten her spirit, she sang a hymn about counting blessings. God had been good to them and she mustn't forget it.

In town, Melanie pulled up in front of Donaldson's store. Sure enough, the flash of pink caught her gaze. The ranger sign was still taped to the front window.

She couldn't explain the chilling anger that swept through her as she got out of the truck, slung her purse over her shoulder and walked into the store. Taking a deep, calming breath, Melanie pulled a shopping cart free and wheeled it toward the canned goods aisle.

It took forty-five minutes to get the dry goods and fresh produce Alfonso liked. Along with the box of homemade chocolate chip cookies she'd made to satisfy his sweet tooth, he should be happy. As she approached the checkout line, she saw Nina Donaldson working the cash register. What was the woman doing here? Nina never worked the weekend, choosing instead to go out on cattle drives with her husband and sons.

Two other customers stood ahead of Melanie and she took the time to breathe deeply and gain her composure. She would bite her tongue, pay for her groceries and leave.

Fifteen minutes later, it was Melanie's turn. Several people stood behind her as she began to unload her cart. "You don't usually work on Saturdays, Nina."

Nina leaned her hip against the counter and rested one hand against her thick waist. "We're shorthanded today. I heard you've been tending the forest ranger's kid."

Caught off guard, Melanie stood there and blinked, holding a box of saltine crackers in one hand, a can of peaches in the other. "I, uh . . . Who told you that?"

"Is it true?"

Melanie's stomach cramped. Dealing with Aaron's rage had made her hate confrontations. She normally didn't pick fights, but she'd become strong enough not to let people push her around, either. "Why does it matter, Nina? What business is it of yours?"

"We don't provide service to forest rangers."

Melanie set the crackers down, forcing herself to meet Nina's eyes. "Do I look like a ranger?"

Nina's lips thinned, her nostrils flaring. Melanie almost laughed, thinking the woman looked like a snorting pig rooting for garbage.

"If you're feeding the ranger's kid, it's my business," Nina said.

"Really? And why is that?"

Nina sneered at her. "Because you're buying food from my store."

"This food is for Alfonso. You've met my herder. A nice man from Peru. You don't have any prejudice against Peruvians, do you?" She sighed impatiently. "Can we please finish our business? I have a busy day."

"Not until I know if you're tending the ranger's brat."

This was getting annoying. And childish. "She's not a brat. She's a sweet little girl, Nina. What harm can she possibly do to you?"

"She's the ranger's kid and we don't give service to rangers. I can understand your wanting a man around. A pretty widow like you, all alone out at your ranch, but you can do better than the ranger, Melanie. Why don't you accept Frank's offer and sell your land to us? Then you and Anne can move into town and you wouldn't have to work so hard."

Something toxic boiled up inside Melanie, much like a nuclear explosion. "How dare you? Just who do you think you are? You have no right to plan my life for me. To tell me what to do with my ranch. I'll never sell Opal Ranch to you. Never."

Melanie stepped back from the counter, gripping the strap of her purse as it dropped off her shoulder and sagged to her elbow. "I'll tell you what, Nina. Since you have enough business already, you can do without mine. You don't own me or anyone else in this town."

And with that, Melanie turned and stormed out of the store. Without looking back, she jerked open the door to her truck, climbed inside, slammed it hard and drove away. She'd made the last stop sign on Main Street and headed out of town before she realized that hot tears of anger ran down her cheeks.

The nerve of that woman! Insinuating that she wanted Scott around her place for anything other than business reasons. Suggesting that she sell her home and the land she dearly loved simply because Frank Donaldson wanted it.

And on top of everything else, Melanie now had no supplies for Alfonso.

When she got home, she burst into the

house, glad the girls weren't there to witness her fury. She dug into her freezer and pulled out two loaves of home-baked bread, then started raiding her pantry.

The creak of the back screen door made her turn around, expecting to see Anne.

"Scott! You startled me."

He smiled at her. "Hi there. I didn't expect you back so soon. How'd it go at the grocery store?"

Her bottom lip quivered and she turned away as more tears spilled down her cheeks. Oh, how she hated for this man to see her cry.

"Mel, are you okay?"

She heard the concern in his voice and felt his warm hands on her shoulders, squeezing gently. She fought the urge to turn in his arms and ask him to hold her. She'd been strong for so long and she wished she could hand some of her burdens over to this kind man. To let him be strong for her.

Then she remembered who he was. And who she was. No, no, no.

She moved away, opening the refrigerator, knowing she was also getting low on provisions for herself and Anne. She needed to buy food. "Nina all but refused to sell me groceries because she found out I'm tending Shelley."

A long, disgruntled breath of air eased past his lips. "I'm sorry, Melanie. This is my fault."

She slammed the fridge door and faced him, rubbing at her damp eyes. "It's not your fault, but it is a problem."

He took a step closer, his hand lifting to tuck a strand of hair back behind her ear. "What can I do to help?"

She looked up into his eyes, so close she could feel the whisper of his breath against her cheek. She opened her mouth to respond, but didn't get the chance. The girls came rushing in, the screen door clapping closed behind them. Scott stepped away.

"Where are the cookies?" Anne's eyes crinkled with disappointment. Her mom had promised to buy chocolate cookies with cream centers.

Melanie bit her bottom lip. She wasn't about to tell her daughter that they could no longer shop at Donaldson's because Shelley was staying with them. No sense in whining about their predicament. Melanie had a job to do and she was determined to do it.

"I didn't get any but I will soon . . . I promise." She brushed a hand across her face. "It looks like it's gonna be a long day.

Three hours to drive to and from Evanston, an hour or so to buy supplies, another three hours to drive up and down the mountain to Alfonso . . . anyone want to ride with me? We can make a day of it." She turned to her daughter. "We can even buy you that new pair of shoes you want to play soccer."

"Yay!" Anne grinned.

"Can we go, too, Dad?" Shelley asked.

Scott folded his arms and leaned against the wall, looking skeptical. Even though he had chores to do here at the ranch, Melanie prayed he said yes. She wanted his companionship today. His presence made her feel better. Stronger. She felt incredibly vulnerable right now and didn't want to be alone with Anne on this long errand.

"I want Shelley to come with me," Anne said.

Melanie chuckled. "It's okay by me."

Melanie felt Scott's eyes resting on her like burning brands. When he spoke, his voice sounded deep and calm. "I owe you for child care this week. I've almost finished repairing the shed and I'd feel better if you let me drive and lift the heavy boxes for you."

What a relief. Melanie released her held breath. Somehow the work of the day didn't seem so burdensome with Scott by her side.

Anne frowned at this, but she didn't object. No doubt her desire to have Shelley along warred with her desire for Scott to remain behind.

"You sure you're up for such a long day?" She bit her tongue, thinking she was stupid to try to talk him out of what she wanted him to do. And yet, she couldn't bring herself to be completely selfish.

He smiled gently, his blue eyes twinkling. "Yeah, and I'll even buy everyone lunch."

Lunch! What a nice treat. It was rare that Melanie didn't have to prepare a meal, and this day might just turn out to be fun.

"Did you get the lambs fed?" Melanie asked.

Anne grinned. "Sure. It goes fast now that Shelley knows what to do and helps me."

"Great. Let's go."

The girls raced ahead with Scott and Melanie following behind. Melanie locked the front door of the house, then bit her tongue when Scott suggested they take his truck.

"We can drive mine," she said. When he threw a dubious glance at her rusty old truck, she hurried on. "It doesn't look like much, but it's got a good engine and it's reliable."

"I just filled my tank with gas." He headed

for his truck, ending their discussion. Funny how he seemed to get his way so easily just by calmly doing things. Aaron would have been screaming profanities at her by this point, making the issue into a big fight that usually ended with her in tears.

As they piled into Scott's truck, Melanie realized that letting him drive was a smarter option. He had a backseat for the girls and Melanie found the truck cab comfortable and roomy.

Anne sat directly behind Melanie with Shelley sitting behind Scott. As they pulled onto the main road, Scott pointed at the corral and yelled, "Beaver."

Melanie and Anne stared at him like he'd gone daft.

He chuckled. "What? You've never played Beaver before?"

They shook their heads.

He looked in the rearview mirror at his daughter. "Shelley, do you want to explain the rules of the game to them?"

"Sure! If you see a colored horse, you call out 'beaver.' That's worth one point. But if you see a white horse, that's worth ten points and you call out 'white horse.' We keep score as we drive along and when we get to our destination, the one with the most points wins."

A laugh burst from Melanie's throat. "The things people come up with to fight off travel boredom."

Scott glanced at her, his handsome mouth curved into a lopsided grin. "So are you in? Or are you afraid I might beat your socks off?"

In response, she pointed at the pristine fields lined by tall, freshly painted white railings surrounding the Donaldsons' ranch. "Beaver, beaver, beaver. That's three points. I'm ahead."

She swiveled in her seat to look back at the girls, whose eyes gleamed with determination. They all stared out the windows, trying to spy a horse as they played the game.

By the time they arrived in Evanston, they were all laughing and calling out the horses they saw before someone else could beat them to it. At the last minute, Anne lucked out with three white horses standing together under a lean-to, which pulled her ahead in points.

"I win!" Anne crowed with delight.

"Ah! No fair," Shelley sulked.

"Yes, my dear, it is fair," Scott said. "You won, Anne. That means you get to decide where we're going to eat lunch today."

Anne looked at Scott and Melanie held her breath. Then the girl gave a half smile and Melanie realized they'd just garnered a very small victory. Anne hadn't argued with him. In fact, the girl was enjoying herself. In spite of Scott being a ranger.

"I'd like to eat at the Burrito Shack, please." She pointed as they approached the restaurant ahead.

And so polite! Maybe having to drive into Evanston was turning out to be worth the effort after all. It had been a long, long time since she and Anne had enjoyed a family outing that didn't entail work.

"Sounds good. I'm starved." Scott pulled into the parking lot.

They ate their lunch, their conversation animated and happy as they discussed how they could change the rules of the Beaver game for their return trip. The day passed most pleasurably as they bought their supplies and headed back to Snyderville.

They stopped by Opal Ranch long enough to put away the perishable groceries and feed the baby lambs again. It was late afternoon by the time they headed up on the mountain.

"Alfonso will be wondering where I am. He expected me by noon," Melanie said.

"He'll understand after we arrive and explain it to him." As they passed Gaylin Canyon, Scott quickly pulled the truck over and shut off the engine without explanation.

"What's the matter?" Melanie asked.

He frowned and seemed distracted as he glanced at the backseat. "You girls can get out of the truck and watch from a distance if you promise to stay with Melanie at all times. Agreed?"

Both girls nodded, not fully understanding what they were agreeing to, but not wanting to be excluded.

Scott got out and they followed, standing beside the truck as he climbed up into the toolbox in the back and retrieved a pair of leather gloves and wire cutters.

"Stay right here. I'll be back."

He sauntered off the road into the sagebrush toward the barbed-wire fence that flowed over the low hills and disappeared into a stand of scrubby juniper. A movement caught Melanie's eye and she couldn't believe what she saw. A deer stood before the fence, its head slung low with its antlers tangled in the barbed wire. She pointed so the girls could see, then lifted them into the back of the truck so they had a better view. True to their promise, they stood beside Melanie, holding her hands.

As Scott approached the wary animal, he spoke in soothing tones. "You sure got yourself into a big mess, didn't you?"

The deer lunged and yanked, blowing hard, nostrils and eyes flared. With its head down, it couldn't move very well. Careful of its hind legs, Scott circled around on the other side of the fence.

"Oh, the poor deer," Anne cooed. "Your dad won't hurt it, will he?"

"Of course not. Dad would never hurt an animal. He helps them," Shelley said, her voice filled with confidence.

"What's he doing, then?"

"His job," Shelley said. "My dad's a forest ranger. Just watch what he's gonna do and you'll be glad he's here."

They watched in silence as Scott pulled on his gloves, then reached for the barbed wire. Already exhausted in its fight to be free of the fencing, the deer jerked and heaved, but couldn't release its horns. Scott wrestled to get a decent grip on the wire, then made several clips with the cutters. The more he freed the animal, the more dangerous it became for Scott. The frightened deer had a greater range of movement and almost kicked Scott off his feet several times. Scott fell, landing hard on his back. Melanie gasped, prepared to run to help, but reticent to leave the girls.

"Hold still, you knucklehead," Scott

gained his feet and yelled when the deer almost speared him with its horns.

Melanie held her breath, her body tense.

With one last clip, Scott freed the deer. In its haste to be liberated, the animal fell to its knees, then lunged up and jumped away, sprinting to freedom in the stand of juniper.

Scott limped back to the truck, holding his left hand with the splint still on his broken finger.

"Are you okay?" she asked.

"Yeah, I just twisted my knee. I'll be fine."

Melanie helped the girls down from the bed of the truck. As she faced Scott, she saw a big gash ripped in his leather glove and blood dripping from a wound on his hand.

"You're hurt." She raced to the truck and reached in the backseat where she'd seen a first aid kit.

"That deer wasn't too appreciative. The barbed wire bit me." He smiled as he pulled off the ruined glove.

Melanie wondered how he could make light of such a deep wound. He was a calm man, which soothed her own nerves. The two girls watched with open mouths as he sat on the back tailgate of the truck and cupped his hand. Blood pooled in his palm and dripped into the dried dirt at their feet.

With somber eyes, Melanie cleaned and wrapped the wound.

"Are you okay, Daddy?" Shelley stood close by in the back of the truck, her little hands gripping her father's right shoulder.

"Sure, pumpkin. I'll be fine." He brushed a finger against her nose.

"Will the deer be okay?" Anne asked him.

He smiled into her eyes, seeming relieved that the young girl was speaking to him. "Yes, he'll be fine. He hadn't been hung up for too long and he wasn't too exhausted. We found him just in time. Much longer, and he could have really injured himself."

Both Anne and Shelley exhaled with relief.

"I'm proud of you two girls," he said. "You did just what I told you to do, and you didn't scream and carry on. Remember, during times of emergency, you need to remain calm, think and act fast. You can panic after the emergency is over."

Both girls nodded, beaming bright smiles at his praise. Melanie liked the way he taught their daughters such a valuable lesson and she couldn't agree more. Scott was good for her and Anne. She liked having him in their lives.

She wrapped gauze around Scott's hand. "The gash is deep. You're going to need stitches."

He shook his head. "I'm not going back to Evanston tonight. I think one trip is plenty for the day. Let's get these supplies delivered to Alfonso. He can help us unload everything."

The girls climbed into the cab of the truck, but Melanie stood looking up at Scott, her mind filled with wonder. "That was amazing what you did."

His eyes softened and he took a step closer, so near she could see the darker navy circle ringing the crystal blue of his pupils. "You're amazing, what you do every day at Opal Ranch and caring for our daughters. I don't know what I'd do without your help."

Melanie swallowed hard. His praise seemed too personal, almost intimate. *Our daughters.* As if they had a bond of blood between them.

Ducking her head, she backed away and took a shuddering breath. "This has been quite a day. I think we'd better get these supplies delivered to Alfonso and go home."

"Yeah." He smiled in understanding.

"Do you want me to drive?"

He shook his head. "I can manage. Come on."

Back in the truck, Melanie stared out her window. Her sharp eyes searched the pastures for the tall larkspur that had been killing her sheep, but she couldn't find any. Instead, she could see where fresh soil had been dug over, uprooting the noxious plants. In other areas, the plants drooped over as if they'd been sprayed with poison to kill them. Obviously, a work crew had been here recently. By the time her sheep herds came to graze this area, the poison would be washed away and the toxic plants would be dead.

She looked over at Scott and a knowing smile spread across his face.

"Thank you," she said.

From the happy glint in his eyes, she could tell he knew what she meant. He'd waited to see if she noticed what he'd done. "You're very welcome, Mrs. McAllister."

And right then, Melanie's opinion of Scott Ennison changed for the better. He had cleaned up the larkspur. He had done a lot of work at her ranch. He had kept his promises to her.

She knew that he still had a long ways to go in meeting with the other ranchers next week, but for now, this was a start.

CHAPTER SEVEN

Scott arrived early at the town hall. The building was just what he expected. A yellow modular home skirted with metal edging to keep animals and the cold out. Turf and shrubs had been planted around the front and sides of the structure with a little toolshed in the back. No doubt the townsfolk had pooled their resources to buy the building. Scott liked that. It meant Snyderville had some community solidarity, although it didn't include him. Yet.

He found the door unlocked and went inside. He'd booked the meeting room with the town mayor, glad the city hadn't charged a fee.

The room smelled musty, as if it hadn't been used recently. The inner walls of the modular had been removed to provide a larger area for meetings and activities. A complete kitchen with a long counter sat off to one side along with a storage room and

141

one restroom. He figured the place could hold about eighty people, but he doubted they'd have more than fifteen ranchers attending tonight's meeting.

Metal chairs stood stacked beside the walls. Without waiting for help, he set to work placing the chairs into rows with walk space along each side and up the center of the room. A small wooden podium and whiteboard sat at the front. There was no microphone, but in such a small room, their voices would carry so everyone could hear. He just hoped there was no shouting tonight. He'd left Shelley over at Karen's house. If Melanie was correct, he'd have to defuse the anger of a bunch of ranchers and he didn't want to expose his daughter to that.

Resting his hands on his hips, he perused the room and tried to settle his nerves. He was ready. He had one chance to prove himself to these people. One chance to win their trust. He must not fail or he would let the entire town down, not to mention irreparably damage his own career.

As people started filing in, he stood close by the door. Ignoring the somber frowns thrown his way, he smiled and tried to shake each person's hand. "Welcome. I'm Scott Ennison."

"Tom Kinsey." A tall, thin man with a receding hairline clasped Scott's hand, meeting his eyes with a direct gaze.

Scott nodded in recognition. "You're running cattle up on Horse Creek."

"That's right. And I'm losing too many from oak poisoning."

"I heard about that from my range assistant and went up there to take a look. I have an idea for a solution."

Tom's bushy brows lifted in surprise. "Is that right? You've been up to Horse Creek?"

Scott nodded. "Two weeks ago."

"Well, that's a miracle. The last ranger just sat in his office. I'd be interested in hearing your idea."

The man turned and walked toward the chairs, taking a seat close to the front. Scott exhaled slowly. That hadn't been so bad.

"I hope you have a solution for me, too."

Scott turned and faced a short man with a long, handlebar moustache and sideburns. Scott reached to take his hand. "I'm Scott Ennison."

"My name's Caleb Hinkle. And Kinsey's cattle keep crossing over onto my allotment and grazing out the bottom land. We need a fence along the boundary."

"I have a suggestion for that problem. We'll talk about it with Tom."

"Good. I reckon we'll be here late tonight, listening to all your suggestions. I just hope you actually follow through for once."

As the man sauntered off, Scott ignored his innuendo. He'd clearly heard the sarcasm in the man's voice, but knew he'd have to let it go and prove he knew how to manage the grazing lands. These problems had been ignored for too long.

By seven o'clock, Scott couldn't believe how many people showed up. He guessed he had forty people in the room, including wives and children who probably couldn't be left home alone. Not all these folks were ranchers. Mrs. Barkley, the part-time post-mistress, was an elderly widow. Ted Winslow had been a rancher years ago, but now owned no livestock and held no grazing permits. Scott realized many people had come out of simple curiosity and nothing more.

They'd come to check out the new ranger.

Scott pulled at the collar of his shirt, then walked to the front of the room so he could begin on time. Starting late might send a message to the ranchers that he didn't respect their time.

He cleared his throat and put a smile in his voice. The people stared at him and he saw the curiosity and uncertainty in their eyes. What if he failed them? What if he couldn't keep his promises to them?

"Thanks for coming out tonight, folks. I appreciate your taking the time to meet with me."

Every person faced forward, their eyes resting on Scott like a ten-ton sledge. A quick scan of the room showed not one friendly face. Some people openly glowered with hostility, while others looked at him with passive expressions. He hoped things didn't turn ugly.

"As most of you know, I'm Scott Ennison, the new district ranger."

Someone snorted and mumbled a derogatory comment. Disgruntled, Scott shifted his weight and began to wonder if this meeting had been a mistake. Maybe he'd underestimated how much the ranchers hated the ranger. But he had a job to do and he wasn't about to back down.

At that moment, Melanie walked in with Anne and sat at the back of the room. She gave him a half smile that went straight to his heart. He couldn't explain why seeing her lifted his spirits and gave him more confidence. For the first time this evening, he didn't feel quite so alone. He nodded at Melanie, but kept his face blank as he cleared his voice and continued with the opening statement he'd practiced at home in front of the bathroom mirror.

"I've already visited with many of you at length, but I thought it might be wise for us to get together and see if there are other problems you may be dealing with. I hope we can work together to figure out some possible solutions. I'm willing to listen and do everything I possibly can to help you out. I grew up on a ranch myself and I believe the land is here for us all to use and take care of for future generations."

Another snort and harrumph.

Scott clenched his hands before forcing himself to relax. His forest supervisor hadn't sent him to this town because the job was easy.

He gestured to Tom Kinsey. "Tom, I understand you have a problem with oak poisoning your cattle when you first go onto the Horse Creek allotment. We had a similar problem in another area where I worked and we solved it by simply feeding the cows the night before they went onto the allotment. Then your cattle won't be so hungry when they first hit the allotment and they won't eat such large quantities of oak and get poisoned."

Tom stared at Scott, who paused to let his suggestion sink in.

"Well, yeah. I reckon that would work. It's a good idea," Tom conceded.

"Good. As to the boundary problem, we can look at the possibility of putting in a fence to separate the pasture adjacent to the Short Bull allotment. I'll have my office manager call and schedule a time when we can meet with Caleb." He cleared his throat. "We could sure use some help building the fence to keep the costs down, though. In this economy, I'm short on manpower."

Caleb's mouth tightened and he sat back, thinking this over. "That sounds reasonable, if Tom will agree."

Tom's face reddened. He nodded and his voice sounded grouchy, but amenable. "All right, I'll make some men available to help build the fence."

"Sounds good. Anyone else have a problem we haven't already discussed?" Scott asked.

Pete Longley, the farrier Scott had met over at Melanie's ranch, lifted his calloused hand. "I'm retired and don't have enough sheep to warrant a herder, so they don't stay where they're supposed to be. With the predator problem, I'm losing a lot of sheep."

Scott hesitated. "How many sheep do you have?"

"Fifty-three."

"What if you put your flock in with another, larger band of sheep? If Mrs. McAllister is amenable, her bands of sheep need a herder and you could pay a portion of the costs to put your sheep with hers."

Pete and Scott looked at Melanie with expectation. Scott hated putting her on the spot. Since she was already friends with Pete, Scott hoped she wouldn't mind adding a small flock in with her bands of sheep.

"Sure, Pete. I'd be happy to help with that," Melanie said.

A cynical laugh burst from Nina Donaldson's mouth. "I'm not surprised. She's tending the ranger's kid. She'll do whatever he wants." She spoke with disgust to the big man sitting next to her. Two younger men who looked to be in their early twenties sat on Nina's other side. Their narrowed eyes made them look just as mean as Nina. Scott thought they must be her sons.

"That's not true." Melanie's eyes narrowed on the other woman. "I think you of all people know I have a mind of my own. But I'm also not a rigid prude who'd do things just to spite myself."

Nina's face flushed red as a rooster wattle. "You don't know what you're talking about."

Melanie rose halfway out of her chair, fire

spitting from her green eyes. If Scott didn't intercede soon, he might have a battle on his hands.

"I'm sorry, Mrs. Donaldson, but we're not here to discuss my daughter's child care. That's my personal business." Scott hated being stern, but he also needed to set a precedent. The ranchers needed to learn what he would and would not tolerate.

Melanie sat back down, her face tight with disapproval.

Nina aimed her barbs at Scott. "You're an outsider. No one wants you here. Why don't you leave?"

Scott took a deep breath and let it go slowly, his pulse racing with anger. "I have a job to do."

He turned away from the woman, deciding not to dignify her with any more responses. Whispers rippled through the crowd as people bent their heads together. Normally, Scott would handle each problem with the people involved. He'd already driven out to most of their ranches to meet with them personally, but he thought this dialogue might also help. He'd been told by his range assistant that Ben Stimpson never met with the ranchers or asked what they needed. It might take some time for the ranchers to get used to Scott's ways.

"Any other issues, or is that it?" Scott asked.

"I doubt our problem will be as easy to solve." A middle-aged rancher sitting next to Nina stood up, his deep bass voice filling the room like thunder. He was a big bear of a man with bushy sideburns, heavy jowls and arms as big as Abrams tanks. "My name's Frank Donaldson and we got eight ranchers grazing the Three Creek allotment and not enough water on the east side."

"That's right! What're you gonna do about that, ranger?" one of Nina's sons chimed in.

So. This was Frank Donaldson. Both Karen and Jim, Scott's range assistant, had warned him about this man. Scott had called and driven out to the Donaldsons' ranch on several occasions, but Nina always claimed that Frank was out working. Frank never returned any of Scott's phone calls. Nina sat next to her husband, her crinkled eyes looking mean as a wolverine.

Tall and burly with red hair, the sons were smaller versions of their father. Scott almost recoiled at the hatred in their eyes. It unsettled him to have complete strangers glaring at him with such loathing — and no matter how many times he told himself that the townsfolk hated the badge he wore — not him personally — it felt like one and the same.

"Yeah, what are you gonna do about it?" Marty Taylor sneered. "We're paying good money for a nice allotment that isn't being grazed because the cattle won't go there without water. The last ranger didn't do anything about it, either."

Funny how they just assumed Scott wouldn't help. He nodded in understanding, determined to ignore their personal slurs. He bit his tongue, trying to be patient in the face of their fury. "I know your cattle are bunching up in places where there is water and overgrazing the land there."

"That's right," Frank growled.

Scott forced a stiff smile onto his face. "It just so happens that I was out at Three Creek several weeks ago, looking things over. Your cattle are definitely grazing to excess in some areas and not using the east side at all. The Forest Service can bring in a D7 crawler tractor with a pipe layer on it and we'll lay plastic pipe about a mile-and-a-half long from the creek down to a water trough we'll put in. That should solve the problem."

"That sounds mighty nice, if you'd do it," Frank yelled. "We've been trying to get Stimpson to put in a water trough for years. That big pot gut never did anything."

Scott tensed at the anger in the man's voice. No doubt this problem had been boiling up inside the ranchers for some time. "There's no need to yell, Mr. Donaldson. I can hear you just fine."

The room burst into shouts as several people stood and started pointing fingers, speaking all at once. Scott didn't even try to keep up with the accusations flying around him. While he realized these people had harsh feelings toward the Forest Service, he couldn't do anything about what Stimpson had or had not done in the past. Now he needed to rebuild these people's trust.

Scott bit his tongue and waited, giving everyone a chance to vent and blow off steam. His mother had taught him that a soft answer turned away wrath and he planned to speak as softly as he could while still being heard.

He glanced at Melanie, finding her in the back, her eyes wide, her normally full lips pressed into a tight line. Anne sat stiffly in her chair as she crossed her arms and glared at Scott. She wore an "I told you so" expression on her face. Of all the people in the room, Scott hated to disappoint this little girl the most. He didn't understand why her opinion meant so much to him, but it did.

The pressure was on.

Scott met Frank's eyes and spoke softly, but clear as a bell. "Mr. Donaldson, I'd like to answer you." The room quieted by slow degrees and Scott tried again, accenting each word. "Mr. Donaldson, I am not Ben Stimpson. If I say I will do something, you can rest assured that I will do it."

"Yeah, right. We've heard that before," Frank snapped.

Scott nodded once, letting his gaze pierce Frank to the core. "I mean what I say."

Frank scoffed and cynicism laced his tone. "And how long will it take you to get this water trough put in? We've been waiting eight years now."

Scott braced himself. Finally he had a jump on the man. This was the fun part and he planned to enjoy every bit of his surprise. "It just so happens that I've already lined up a D7 dozer with a pipe layer and the crew is working on the springhead right now."

Dead silence filled the room. Scott waited, letting his words sink in.

"You mean you've already started the work?" Marty's voice sounded skeptical.

"That's right." Scott inwardly laughed with delight. He'd caught them off guard, doing work before they asked him for it.

He'd planned it this way so they would see that he was serious about helping them all he could.

Frank's mouth dropped open and he stared with disbelief. "Your crew is already working at Three Creek."

A statement, not a question. Why wouldn't they believe him?

"Yes," Scott said. "I inspected their work myself just yesterday. The D7 will be here on Monday morning, so they'll start to make more progress then. Later, we'll have a pad prepared for a cement slab and we'll put in the water trough."

"But . . . but you — ?" Frank sputtered.

"The work should be finished within four weeks," Scott hurried on. "I'm sorry it can't be done sooner, but we'll need time to bury the pipe and let the cement slab dry before we can bring the water down from the creek."

Marty shook his head. "I can't believe it."

Scott didn't smile. He wanted to teach these people that when he said something, he meant it. He wouldn't joke about something this important. "Why don't you ride out to Three Creek and take a look for yourself? I'd be happy to give you a tour of the project."

Frank sat down, a big woof of air escaping

his chest. The dumbfounded glare on his face remained. When his wife leaned in to whisper in his ear, he brushed her away impatiently and rested his clenched hands on his thighs.

Whew! Thank goodness Donaldson was cowed for the time being. Scott was not a small man, but he had no desire to tangle with Frank's beefy fists.

"Now I have a request for you ranchers." Scott paused, hoping to gain their attention. "Many of your cattle are moving into the creeks and just staying there. They're destroying the creek bottoms. You need to move your cattle periodically so they don't permanently damage the creeks. My staff will be checking the creek beds to make sure this is done, so I'll expect you to take care of it."

Frank popped back out of his seat with a roar; not an easy feat for such a big man. "We can't go in and round up our cattle and move them every day."

Frank was being difficult for no reason. Scott had made a reasonable request. A request that would benefit everyone. He took a deep breath, forcing himself to speak calmly in the face of Frank's belligerence. "Mr. Donaldson, you won't have to go in very often to move your cattle. Once every few days should help, if you place your salt correctly. I would like to ride out with you to see where we think the salt should be laid. Can we set that up in the next week?"

"That's not an unreasonable request, Frank," Marty said. "You send your sons out to check on your cattle every few days anyway. We all do. It's nothing to move our cattle out of the creek beds so they aren't ruined. We can put our salt away from the creeks so the cattle will move."

The glower on Frank's face darkened. Scott could tell this man didn't like being told what to do by anyone. Period. It might take a great deal of time to win Donaldson over, if ever.

"Mr. Donaldson?" Scott wanted a commitment from the man. Right now.

"All right," Donaldson growled.

"Good. My office manager will contact you to set it up." Deep down, Scott knew it was in his best interest to ignore the man's foul temper. Although he could certainly handle the fact that the Donaldsons had refused to sell groceries to him, he didn't want Melanie hurt in the process. He didn't understand why he felt so protective of her and Anne, but he did. He could easily retaliate against the Donaldsons if he liked. Scott had the power to make Donaldson's life miserable, but Scott wasn't a vindictive man. He didn't want to make enemies. He wanted to defuse all the anger the past ranger had stirred up. Scott's reputation depended on his success.

"And one more request." Scott hesitated. "You sheep ranchers need to keep your herds moving along the roadway leading up to your allotments. All our permittees use the driveway and it's being overgrazed. Don't let your bands of sheep linger there. The Forest Service will be patrolling the driveway to help you keep your sheep moving."

Patrolling was a better word than *policing*. Scott didn't want to be hard-nosed, but he needed to let the sheep ranchers know they could no longer overgraze the driveway the way they had in the past.

The conversation continued as they resolved other, simpler issues. Some of the ranchers appeared willing to give Scott a chance to prove himself. Others, like Frank Donaldson, could be belligerent, critical and nasty. It would take longer to win them over.

By the time everyone left, it was ten o'clock and Scott felt drained of energy. He began stacking chairs to put them away before he went to pick up Shelley. No doubt she had fallen asleep. He'd get her tucked into bed and then make plans for tomorrow's workday. He also needed to move sprinkler pipe for Melanie tomorrow night and start preparing to mow her hay.

He sighed, weary to the bone.

As he turned, Melanie caught his eye, still sitting at the back of the room. Anne lay asleep on the floor, her jacket scrunched beneath her head for a pillow.

Melanie stood and met him halfway across the room. He put his hands in his pants pockets to keep from reaching out and hugging her. "Hi . . . I didn't know you were still here."

"Yeah, I wanted to talk to you before I went home." Her smile stole his breath. He sure needed a friend right now.

"What about?" he asked.

"I have my own grazing problem, but I decided to wait until everyone else was gone before I addressed it with you."

"What? No yelling at me?" He chuckled.

She gave a shy smile. "Of course not. Unless you're Nina Donaldson. I'm sorry about that. She really got under my skin tonight. Yelling isn't usually my style."

Thank goodness. The longer he knew this woman, the more he admired her. He leaned one shoulder against the wall, looking down at her, enjoying the pretty pink flush on her face. "So what can I help you with, Mrs. McAllister?"

"My herder is bedding our sheep in one place too often so the land is being over-grazed. We need more bedding grounds."

Her honesty intrigued him. Most ranchers waited for him to notice that they were abusing the land before they stopped. Maybe she really did care about preserving the land for her daughter to use when she was grown up.

"How about if we lay crushed salt out so your sheep will be on it before they start grazing in the mornings? You can haul the salt in on pack animals and lay it down in different places to draw your sheep to new bedding grounds. They'd naturally gravitate to where you want them to go."

Her eyes brightened. "That would definitely work. My herder can put the salt out after we find some suitable places."

"Absolutely. I can help you find some good places next week." He smiled wide, anticipating riding with her up on the mountain. He breathed deeply of her warm, clean scent and wished he dared touch the long, soft strands of hair framing her face.

"And just one more problem."

"Yes?" he prodded.

"Coyotes. They're bad this year. You

already know about the grizzly, but coyotes are bad all year long."

"I know. After my run-in with the bear, I contacted the State Game and Fish Department to see if they can help us with the problem."

"And?"

He shrugged. "They said they'd see what they could do. But don't worry. I've called them three times now. I figure if I nag them often enough, they'll get tired of me and come do something about it just to shut me up."

She laughed, the sound musical to his ears.

"Can I walk you out?" he asked as she turned and headed toward Anne.

"Sure."

Without being asked, he lifted Anne and carried the girl outside. The warm night air smelled of honeysuckle. The single porch light over the doorway of the town hall showed them the way and he enjoyed the view as Melanie hurried ahead to unlock her truck. Lucky for him, Anne didn't wake up as he slid her onto the front seat, then backed away while Melanie buckled the girl in and closed the door.

"You handled the ranchers surprisingly well tonight," she told him.

He took a step closer, her praise pleasing him enormously. "I did?"

"Yes, very well. Thanks again for everything."

"You're welcome." Another step and he wished he could —

"See you tomorrow."

She brushed past him and he opened the door for her. She climbed inside before closing the door and starting the engine.

Scott stood back while she pulled out of the gravel parking lot. He watched until her taillights faded. A lonely feeling enveloped him. How he wished he dared ask Melanie out on a date, like real grown-ups. But he'd seen how Nina had attacked Melanie and he didn't want to give her any more trouble than she already had.

He shook his head. It was time for him to forget the pain of his divorce. Time for him to get on with his life. No matter how busy he was, he never got over the emptiness in his heart. But he needed to focus on Shelley and his career. Nothing else must distract him from those goals.

Tonight had been successful. He had listened to the ranchers' concerns and offered reasonable solutions. Now he needed to go to work. He planned to meet with his assistants and crewmen first thing in the morning to make more assignments.

If he didn't keep his promises, he'd lose all his credibility with the ranchers. And with Melanie. It was that simple.

CHAPTER EIGHT

On Sunday morning, Melanie arrived early at church so she could set out some pictures for her Sunday school class lesson. Anne helped her, placing a picture of the Savior on a small tabletop easel.

"I want to show Shelley my new dress. You think she'll be here today?" Anne ran a hand over the skirt of her dainty blue dress. She'd insisted that Melanie curl her hair the night before and pull it back with a matching ribbon this morning. Melanie was pleased to see how hard her daughter was trying to act like a refined young lady instead of a rough tomboy. More and more, she believed having Shelley around was good for her daughter.

"You look beautiful, but I doubt she'll be here. Maybe we should invite her again." So far, Scott had ignored Melanie's offers to pick up Shelley and bring her to church with them. She'd invited him to come along, but he always made some gruff excuse.

"Her dad won't let her come," Anne grouched.

"That doesn't mean we should stop trying. The Lord loves all His children."

"Even forest rangers?"

Melanie hid a chuckle. "Especially forest rangers. It can't be easy for Scott and Shelley, living here in Snyderville where they don't have many friends. But Scott's working hard to prove himself to everyone. You should give him some credit for that."

Anne's brow furrowed with thought. Melanie couldn't help remembering the rancher meeting when Scott had stood up and helped find resolutions to some of their grazing problems. He hadn't accepted all the responsibility, but patiently demanded that the ranchers do their part. She'd been impressed by his knowledgeable concessions. And later, when he'd walked her out to her truck, she'd found herself thinking that he was the most handsome man she'd ever —

Enough of that!

Gathering her papers and a roll of tape, she urged Anne toward the door. "Come on, sweetie. We'd better get into the chapel before the meeting starts."

They hurried to find a bench where they sat alone. Nina Donaldson sat playing the organ and soft music filtered over the air, setting the stage for reverence.

As the meeting was about to start, the discordant sound of Nina skipping several notes alerted Melanie that something was wrong. She looked over her shoulder as Scott and Shelley Ennison walked into the chapel and took a seat in a back pew. The murmur of people went deathly quiet. Everyone turned to stare at Scott and his daughter.

Looking as confident as ever, he smiled and nodded to several people before he crossed his long legs. He dropped an arm over Shelley's shoulders, a protective gesture that only Melanie might detect. Not seeming to care if she wrinkled her pink taffeta dress, Shelley leaned against her father's side and hid part of her face against his pinstriped suit. Her blue eyes widened as she looked at all the people staring at her and Scott. She didn't seem to have her father's confidence. In that moment, Melanie's respect for Scott increased. How did he have the fortitude to sit calmly in the face of so many glares of anger? In the house of the Lord, no less.

He was an outsider here. He didn't belong. And yet, she wanted him here. She couldn't wait to see his truck pull up out front of her house. To talk to him. To be near him. To know he was there for her whenever she was so tired she could barely stand the thought of going outside to move another sprinkler pipe.

He looked handsome in a pristine white shirt and red tie, his black hair slightly damp and slicked back with gel. In place of his scuffed cowboy boots, he wore shiny, black wingtips. Melanie had never seen him dressed in anything other than a ranger uniform or blue jeans. Even then, he'd been a startlingly handsome man. But now, with his lean cheeks freshly shaven, and a gleam in his eyes, he looked like he'd just walked off the pages of a glossy magazine cover.

One thought pounded Melanie's mind. What was he doing here? Why had he come? He'd made it clear that he had no time for the Lord. Surely he hadn't had a change of heart so soon. Maybe he didn't really mean what he'd said about abandoning God. Maybe —

Anne nudged her as the congregation began to sing a hymn. Realizing that she was staring, Melanie whirled around and faced front. She'd completely missed the announcements and the chorister standing up to lead the music.

Sharing a hymnal with her daughter, she went through the motions of singing. What on earth was the matter with her? She couldn't explain her interest in Scott. He was a curiosity because he was the ranger — that was all. Her attraction to the man couldn't run deeper than that.

Or could it?

Following the meeting, she planned to welcome Scott to church, but he disappeared. In her Sunday school classroom, she hid her surprise when Shelley walked in with Anne.

"Welcome, Shelley." Melanie smiled. "Did your father go to the adult class?"

Shelley shrugged. "I think so."

"Hey! She's not gonna be in our class, is she?"

Melanie glanced at Bart Donaldson. A small replica of his burly father, Bart was also Frank and Nina's youngest son. The baby of the family. And spoiled rotten.

It never occurred to Melanie that Shelley might not be accepted at church. Wasn't this the one place where all God's children should be welcomed?

"Bart, don't stand on the chair. Get down right now. Of course Shelley's in our class." Melanie faced the entire class of eleven children and silently groaned. Keeping this many ten- and eleven-year-olds reverent while she tried to teach them about the Savior might prove challenging. "Children, I want you all to welcome Shelley Ennison to our class. She's new in town and we're happy to have her here."

"No, we're not." Bart wrinkled his nose. "Something smells like . . . like the Forest Service."

He sniffed the air with repugnance, turning toward Shelley. "Yuck! It's you. You stink."

Shelley's eyes filled with tears and she sniffed her pretty dress, as if to verify what the boy said. "I took a bath last night. I don't stink."

Her voice quivered with uncertainty.

"Yes, you do. You stink like the Forest Service. Smelly Shelley!"

"That's enough, Bart! Don't call names," Melanie said.

The damage was done. The other children burst into laughter, pointing and yelling. "Smelly Shelley! Smelly Shelley!"

Shelley burst into tears, hiding her eyes behind her hands. This distressed Anne, who rarely held back what she was thinking. The girl whirled around and faced Bart.

"Knock it off, Bart. No one smells worse

than you," Anne said. "I've never seen you walk through a corral yet without stepping in a cow pie, even if there's only one cow pie for a mile around. You always seem to find it."

"I do not," Bart snapped back.

"Do, too!"

"That's enough!" Melanie demanded as she grasped Bart by the arm and gently pulled him down into a sitting position. "You will all sit still and not say one more word, or I will send you out to join your parents. Understood?"

That shut up Bart and the other kids. Nina Donaldson hated the forest ranger, but she claimed she was a religious woman and Melanie doubted she'd take kindly to her son getting booted out of Sunday school class for calling names. Of course, if Nina knew it was because Bart had teased the ranger's daughter, the woman might make an exception. Melanie wasn't sure what to think at this point. She did know that she would not accept such behavior in her class.

Melanie wrapped her arm around Shelley and pulled her close. "I need a helper today. Will you hold up the pictures for me, sweetheart?"

Shelley sniffled, rubbed her wet eyes and sat between Melanie and Anne.

Melanie had prepared a lesson about faith, but figured these kids needed something else today. Instead, she said a silent prayer asking the Lord for help, then launched into a sweet message about the Good Samaritan and accepting others. Luckily, she had a picture of the Good Samaritan in her lesson box to give Shelley to hold up.

Bart glared the entire time, his arms folded across his wide chest, his bottom lip curled with repugnance. At least he didn't trouble Shelley anymore, but Melanie was careful to keep the girl beside her and Anne until after class ended. Then she gathered up her lesson materials and walked with the girls outside to find Shelley's dad. Bart wasn't above getting into a fistfight at church, and Melanie planned to deliver Shelley safely to her father before leaving her alone.

Shelley gazed up at her as their heels tapped against the cement walk path. "Melanie, why don't the other kids like me?"

"They don't know you. Sometimes people are scared of people they don't know."

"You mean like the Good Samaritan?" she asked.

"Exactly. That's why some people refused to help the man from Jerusalem. They were afraid, but it was more than that. Samaritans believed it was unclean for them to touch a man from Jerusalem." When Shelley furrowed her brow in confusion, Melanie tried her best to explain. "You see, most people of Samaria hated people from Jerusalem. But the Good Samaritan helped his neighbor, knowing he could be ostracized by his own people for doing so."

"What's ostrich sized?"

Melanie laughed. "Ostracized. The people of Samaria could have sent the Good Samaritan away for helping a man from Jerusalem. He normally wouldn't have had anything to do with a man from Jerusalem. The Samaritan and his family might have ended up starving to death for what he did. So he took a big chance by helping out."

"But why'd he do it?" Shelley probed.

"Because he was obeying a greater law. The law of Christ, which says everyone is our neighbor and we are each our brother's keeper."

"Even if we don't like them?" Anne interjected.

"Absolutely."

"So we should give our enemy food if the general store refuses to sell them groceries?" Shelley said.

"Yes, honey. If that's what it takes. The Lord requires us to forgive all men and to love our enemies." Tears pricked the backs of Melanie's eyes as she recounted the deep meaning of the story. She'd never considered herself a Good Samaritan, but she realized Scott and Shelley were her neighbors, too. She believed God expected her to care for them all she could, in spite of their being natural enemies.

A testament to God's love for all mankind burned deep within her heart. She didn't consider Scott her enemy; helping him was the right thing to do, even though she could be ostracized by others within her community.

"Bart's a twit. Don't you let him worry you one bit," Anne said with disgust.

"Anne, remember I spoke to you about name calling?" Melanie reminded him.

"But I didn't think that included twits like Bart."

"It includes everyone," she said.

As they walked to the parking lot, Melanie listened to the swish of Shelley's taffeta dress and took a deep, settling breath. What a workout! She felt as though she had just wrestled a bear, physically and emotionally. When she came to church today, she never expected to learn such an important lesson. But she needed to set an example for her class. She felt in awe of Christ's teachings.

Who would have thought a Sunday school class of ten- and eleven-year-olds would teach her so much?

"Why'd you let Bart push you around like that?" Anne directed her question at Shelley.

"I . . . I don't —" Confusion crossed Shelley's delicate features.

Anne leaned closer, as if sharing some special information. "My dad always said you have to stand up to bullies. Don't let Bart push you around or he'll figure he's allowed to do it and make your life miserable."

Melanie smiled, grateful that some things Aaron had said to their daughter were valuable life lessons. How odd that Aaron had been so intimidating, yet he'd taught their daughter to stand up for herself. Melanie couldn't help wondering how long before Anne would have become cowardly and shy if her father had started slapping her around.

Shelley was a gentle soul and Melanie hated that the girl was learning some difficult lessons, but decided not to reprimand Anne for pointing these things out. Life was hard and it would do Shelley some good to learn to toughen up a bit, especially since her father was in a difficult line of work that might continue to bring censure from others.

"Do you see your dad?" she asked.

Both Shelley and Anne craned their heads, searching the parking lot for some sign of Scott.

"There he is." Anne pointed.

Scott had been talking with one of the men. When he saw them, Melanie's throat constricted. The sight of him sauntering toward them in his pristine suit stole her breath.

"Hello, ladies," he greeted them all with a wide smile, his blue eyes sparkling. "You're looking beautiful this Sabbath morning, Mrs. McAllister."

The rich timbre of his voice sent waves of warmth up Melanie's spine. His gaze moved over her flower-print dress and open-toed high heels. She'd painted her toenails light pink and he stared at them for several heartbeats. Melanie shivered.

Anne hung back, but at least the hatred had left her eyes. Maybe today's lesson had sunk in. Maybe she was getting used to Scott and learning to trust him.

Melanie forgot to breathe. She was still woman enough to know when a man found her attractive and she couldn't help feeling pleased by his greeting. "Did you enjoy your church meetings?"

"They were okay. How are you, hon?" He rested his hand on Shelley's shoulder and met her eyes.

Melanie's heart sank. Now that he had finally come to church, she had hoped to see more enthusiasm in him.

"Daddy, they said I stink and called me Smelly Shelley," the girl said.

Scott frowned down at her. "Who did?"

Melanie explained, making sure he knew she hadn't approved and had put an immediate stop to the teasing. "I'm sorry, Shelley. Don't you listen to such nonsense. You're always welcome in my class." She tilted her head to look up at Scott. "In fact, Shelley was my big helper today. She held up the pictures and got out the pencils and paper for the other kids."

Melanie purposefully neglected to tell Scott that most of the kids refused to use the pencils because they might be "contaminated" by the Forest Service since Shelley had touched them first.

"I helped a little," Anne chimed in.

Melanie wrapped her arm around her daughter. "Yes, you did. I was lucky to have such good helpers today."

Both girls beamed at the praise, then moved off together, chasing after a butterfly.

Scott took a step nearer to Melanie. "Thanks for that. I appreciate your looking out for Shelley."

"It was my pleasure." And she meant it. "I can't help being surprised that you came to church today. It was great to see you and Shelley walk through the door. You must have had a change of heart."

Okay, hopeful thinking. She awaited his response, not sure why it meant so much to her that he give up his grudge against God.

"I did it for Shelley." His voice sounded flat. "She needs to make friends and I thought maybe the kids would go easier on her here at church."

"Then you didn't come because —"

He shook his head. "I don't need God in my life, Melanie. But I do need Shelley. She's all I have left and I want her to be happy."

A lump formed in Melanie's throat. She didn't like the way this conversation was going, but she should have known his motives couldn't be simple. "But I already offered to pick Shelley up and bring her to church with Anne and me. Why did you bring her if you don't want to be here?"

He brushed a hand against his face and looked away, his eyes filled with a bit of guilt. "I figured some of the ranchers might change their view of me if they saw me in church. It couldn't hurt."

Something cold gripped Melanie's heart. "So you're using God to get in good with the ranchers?"

He met her gaze without flinching, the guilt gone, his beautiful blue eyes chilling her to the core. "That's right. I don't need God for anything else. If it softens my relationship with the local ranchers, I'll take all the help I can get."

Melanie frowned. "Scott, that just seems so . . ."

"What?"

"Dishonest," she said.

"Dishonest to use God?"

"Yes." A sick feeling settled in her stomach. She didn't know why she bothered discussing this topic with him. His well-being and relationship with God weren't her business. And yet she couldn't let it go. Caring for him felt like water running through her fingers. She couldn't get a grip on it. Why did she like this man so much?

He flashed a smile. "I also figure if God's looking for me, this is a good place to be."

That sounded promising. "I've found that God's always there for us. It's we who stop looking for Him, not the other way around. But I also think the Lord pulls back and waits for us to realize that we need Him, just as any loving parent waits for his child to learn lessons and figure things out on his own."

Scott took a deep breath before letting it go. "There was a time when I sought out God, but He turned His back on me."

At least Scott hadn't said he didn't believe in God. They could work with that. She was certain Scott just needed time to heal and forgive himself and his former wife for divorcing him. In time, Scott would come to realize that the Lord hadn't abandoned him. "Are you sure the Lord turned his back on you, or just didn't give you the answer you wanted to hear?"

He didn't respond, but his gaze darkened.

"The Lord gives us free agency to choose our own actions. He won't interfere if we make up our minds, and He won't take away our free agency to choose." She smiled gently at Scott. "God allows us to learn from our own mistakes, but He's still there to help soften the blows."

Scott's brow furrowed and he shrugged. "It doesn't matter anymore. Would you rather I was a hypocrite and said I wanted God in my life when I really don't?"

That stopped her. Wasn't everyone a hypocrite to some extent? Including her. "I

178

think we all need repentance. No one is perfect, Scott. We all make mistakes. But it isn't our place to judge others. We each have trials and obstacles we are fighting to overcome. Our progression of faith is personal, between us and God. I just hate to see you like this. You're a good man and yet you could be so much more if you'd let the Lord help you."

A flash of pain filled his eyes, then was gone, but not before she realized that she'd hurt him with her words. He drew away, looking for Shelley.

Melanie had been the bully this time. That water had run through her fingers and splattered on her toes. While she meant to share her own heartfelt love of the Lord with Scott, and open his heart as well, she never wanted to make him feel unworthy or inadequate. She couldn't forget Scott's gentleness with animals and his attempts at kindness to Anne, but she liked being single. Liked being free of contention in her home. To make her own choices without fear of reprisal from a domineering man. Scott was a strong, determined man. She could never have a permanent relationship with him. Her heart couldn't take it when he finally left Snyderville.

"Nice talking to you, Mrs. McAllister.

Shelley, let's go," he called before glancing back at Melanie. "I won't be dropping Shelley off at your place tomorrow. I'm going up on the mountain and thought I'd take her with me."

What did he mean? "Scott, please don't take offense. I never meant to —"

"It's just for a day or two. I'll bring her over on Wednesday, okay?"

"Okay." Relief flooded her and all she could do was nod. She'd really stepped in it this time, hurting him when she wanted nothing more than to encourage him to accept God in his life. So much for missionary work. She'd made a complete mess of her efforts.

"See you Wednesday," she called and waved as he sauntered toward his truck.

Wednesday was only three days away, and yet it felt like a century. She'd gotten used to having Shelley and Scott around her place. It seemed natural, working together, fetching cold refreshments for him and the girls. The thought of not seeing him anymore left her feeling empty inside. Like her world had tilted and might never be right again.

She told herself it wasn't because she was attracted to Scott. She just felt accountable for damaging his relationship with the Lord.

And Anne was so happy playing with Shelley. Even if they were two complete opposites, the girls needed each other.

As Melanie walked across the lush church lawn with Anne, she realized that she had to do something about this awkward situation. Before Scott decided she wasn't fit to watch Shelley anymore. And she had to do it fast.

CHAPTER NINE

The next morning, Scott took Shelley and drove up to the Snyder Mountains with Jim Tippet, his range assistant. Together, they unloaded their three horses from the trailer, then headed across the Three Creek allotment. They rode slow, conscious of Shelley. She'd become a good rider, but she could easily be thrown off if her horse stumbled or got spooked for some reason.

It'd been a challenge to coordinate the equipment and manpower for this project. Scott thought that was probably one reason Ben Stimpson had resisted pursuing the job.

Sitting astride his horse, Scott paused to watch the D7 work. The roar of the engine filled the air, along with dust and the buzz of chain saws as several men cleared bigger trees out of the way. He chuckled when he saw Shelley covering her ears to block out the loud racket.

The wide tracks of the D7 distributed the

weight and gave the machine better traction as the driver lowered the angling blade and pushed brush and earth out of the way.

"You've done a good job coordinating this project, Jim. We're right on schedule," Scott yelled above the noise and smiled at his assistant.

Jim nudged Scott and pointed to the hillside as he called back. "Looks like we've got company."

Shielding his eyes from the bright sun, Scott saw the unmistakable figure of Frank Donaldson standing on a hilltop with his two eldest sons and another man he thought was Marty Taylor. The men had several pairs of binoculars, looking down to survey the work. Knowing he was being watched, Scott smiled and waved. He reined in his horse and headed toward the hill to ride up, but the men turned and got in their truck. Being on horseback, Scott couldn't catch them. He stopped and watched as dust from their passing vehicle sifted across the road.

"Now they know I mean business," he spoke beneath his breath.

"What?" Jim spoke above the roar of engines.

"Nothing. Let's take a ride over to the driveway." He spoke loud, turning to smile at Shelley. "You doing okay, pumpkin?"

She heard him even with her hands crushed over her ears. "Yes, but it's too noisy here."

"Let's go." They rode away, speaking again once they could hear themselves think.

"I'll come up again tomorrow, just to see how the work progresses," Jim promised.

"Good. If possible, I'd like to stay right on schedule."

He figured Marty and the Donaldsons were just aching for him to fail. Which made him even more determined to succeed. Scott wasn't here to make friends, but he did intend to do his job. And to do it right.

When they arrived at the driveway, they stopped and ate their sack lunches. Allowing their horses to graze a short distance away, they sat on the ground and leaned their backs against the trunk of a fallen juniper. They enjoyed the spectacular, panoramic view. Caleb Hinkle's sheep filled the meadow below, on their way up to the mountain. The main driveway to the Snyder Mountains was a grassy area leading up to the various grazing allotments. Almost all the ranchers used the through-way. Lingering here with herds of sheep or cattle only made the grazing problem worse. When Scott had told the ranchers that the Forest Service would be patrolling the area to ensure the herds kept moving, he meant it.

"Hey! There's Anne and Melanie." Shelley pointed as Melanie parked her truck on the side of the dirt road.

An unexpected feeling of euphoria pulsed through Scott's veins. After yesterday, he thought perhaps he should put some distance between himself and the lovely widow. She loved God and he wanted nothing to do with religion. She wanted something from him that he couldn't give her.

It did no good. For some reason, he couldn't get her out of his mind. Nor could he stop thinking about what she'd said about the Lord always being there, waiting for His children to ask for His help.

If Scott ever needed help, it had been during his divorce. But Melanie was right. Allison had decided to leave him and abandon their daughter for another man. God hadn't forced her to do such a thing. In fact, maybe the Lord had blessed Scott by letting him keep Shelley with him. If not for his little girl, Scott didn't know how he would have kept his sanity. She'd come to mean everything to him, teaching him that family was more important than anything else.

And maybe God had even sent the McAllisters into their lives. To help make things easier for them here in Snyderville.

That thought caused Scott to pause. Could it be that the Lord wanted him and Shelley to be with Melanie and Anne? Certainly something to think about.

Shelley hopped up and took off like a shot, waving her arms. "Anne! Anne!"

"Looks like Shelley's got herself a good friend," Jim said.

"Yeah, the girls are almost inseparable."

"The mother's not bad, either. A beautiful woman. And she's one of the few ranchers who seem to have accepted you." Jim chuckled.

Yeah, Scott silently agreed. As Melanie stepped out of her truck, the breeze swept wisps of hair around her face. Remembering her yesterday in her dainty dress, he stared at her slim legs encased in faded blue jeans and marveled at how lovely she looked no matter what she wore.

"Guess I'll go have a chat with Caleb, then we can head back to town." Jim stood and headed for his horse.

Likewise, Scott stood and brushed dust off his pants before stowing the remains of their lunch in his saddlebags. Then he walked over to meet Melanie.

"Hi there." She sounded a bit breathless, bracing an elbow against the truck.

Pushing his hat back on his head, he

couldn't help returning her bright smile. "I didn't expect to see you here on the mountain today."

"Actually, I came looking for you. Your office said we might find you here."

He tilted his head. "Is everything okay?"

"Yeah, I just wanted to give you this." She handed him a paper. "Shelley said she wanted to play soccer with Anne. Signups are due tomorrow afternoon and since you won't be bringing Shelley over to the house until Wednesday, I was afraid that she might not be able to join in time." She cleared her throat. "I was hoping you would complete the form and I could turn it in for you tomorrow and then take Shelley with Anne when practice starts on Thursday."

"Ah, I see." He scanned the enrollment application, her consideration touching his heart. Few people in this community would have done so much for him and Shelley. Reaching into his front shirt pocket, he withdrew a pen. He laid the paper on the front fender of her truck and quickly filled out the application, but paused when he reached the part about emergency contacts. "Do you mind if I put your name here?"

She looked over his shoulder before shaking her head. "Of course not. I've taken you to the hospital before. I'm sure I could do it for Shelley, if the need arises."

He laughed. "I think you know my insurance number better than I do."

He reached into his back pants pocket to withdraw his checkbook, filled out a check for the required enrollment fees, signed the form and handed it all back to her. "Here you go. Thanks for coming all the way up here for this. Shelley mentioned it to me, but I forgot to ask you about it. She's very excited about playing soccer."

"It's no problem."

She glanced over at Caleb and Jim, who were deep in conversation as they gestured toward the mountain. When she spoke, Scott heard caution in her voice. "I passed by the Donaldsons on my way up here. Is everything okay?"

Good. News would soon spread throughout Snyderville that Scott had kept his promise. "Yep. The backhoe started digging trench over at Three Creek and they were there to watch."

"I'm so glad." She smiled. "Maybe that will shut them up. I'm tired of their constant whining. Next time, they'll listen and trust you more."

He thought the same thing, but her vote of confidence reached into his very core. Why did this woman seem to trust and support him so much? He'd only known her a handful of weeks, yet he felt closer to her than he'd ever felt to Allison. He thought he'd never meet a woman like Melanie and now he feared it was too late. They each came with too much baggage. Too much hurt and distrust. Love had passed him by a long time ago.

"I'll be a bit late tonight to do my chores at your place," he said.

She blinked. "You're planning to come over tonight to work?"

"Sure. I owe you for child care." He leaned nearer, catching her warm scent and thinking himself crazy for enjoying it so much.

"But I didn't think you'd be there since you didn't bring Shelley over today. You don't owe me, Scott. In fact, I owe you."

"It was our agreement. I'd like to mow the hay in your south pasture tonight."

She waved a hand. "I can have Ernie Murphy take care of that. He said he can come on Friday to do it."

The thought made him feel a bit territorial. He'd moved the sprinklers and watched the hay grow. He wanted to mow it. "Nope, I promised to take care of it and I will."

"If you're sure. I'll call Ernie and tell him not to come. We'll see you later." She waved to get Anne's attention.

Scott and Shelley watched as the McAllisters climbed into Melanie's truck and left, then Shelley released a long sigh. "I wish Anne was my sister and Melanie was my mom. Then we wouldn't have to leave each other all the time."

Stunned, Scott stared at his daughter. "What about your own mom? I thought you missed her."

She looked up at him, his gentle, sensitive daughter's eyes filled with sadness. A look that mirrored his own feelings. "I do, but I know she's never coming back, Dad. Melanie's different. She'd never leave us. And Anne's my BFF."

"BFF?"

"Best friend forever."

He smiled at that, thinking how wise his child had become. But making Melanie his wife and Anne his stepchild were a far stretch of the imagination. Up until this moment, he hadn't allowed himself to even think about that. But hearing his own longings voiced out loud by Shelley almost staggered his mind.

"I'm glad you and Anne love each other," he said. "But I hope you realize there really can't be anything more between Melanie and me."

"Why not? Karen married Mike after she divorced her first husband. They've been married for years and raised each other's kids. Why can't you do the same thing with Melanie? Then Anne and I wouldn't be half dogies anymore."

Oh, man. Talk about a complicated question . . . "First, we would have to be in love. And second, Anne would need to accept me, which she doesn't. And third, my career will eventually force me to make a transfer someplace else. You'll have to go with me." He gazed down at his daughter. "We won't be living in Snyderville forever, Shelley. I hope you realize that."

He headed for his horse, hoping she'd drop the subject. Hoping she wouldn't say anything that made him feel worse about the situation than he already did.

"I don't want to leave Snyderville. I want to stay here. Anne just doesn't know you well enough yet."

Yet. As if more time might turn Anne's animosity toward him into acceptance and not make him an evil forest ranger anymore. Scott couldn't allow either himself or his daughter to dwell on this topic. It would bring them nothing but pain.

"Look, honey. I don't want you to think that Melanie and I can be anything other than friends." He finished too abruptly, as if trying to convince himself.

She frowned, not seeming to like that answer. He didn't give her the chance to question him further as he lifted her up on her pony, handed her the reins, then turned to step up on his own mount.

"It's been a long day. Let's go home." He nudged his horse with his heels and headed off toward the Forest Service truck and horse trailer.

Once they had the horses loaded, Jim drove them back to Snyderville. Shelley sat between the two men, staring out the window as she brooded on her own thoughts. She seemed lost and so vulnerable that Scott reached over and took her hand in his, but she jerked away.

That hurt.

What could he say to soften her dejection? He hoped she'd give up any ideas about him and Melanie getting hitched. Turns out they were both becoming too attached to the McAllisters. But deep inside, he couldn't help asking himself some questions that seemed to haunt him lately.

Like why did they ever have to leave? And why couldn't they stay?

Two hours later, Scott and Shelley arrived

at Opal Ranch. He didn't wait to greet Melanie before he headed out to the barn, forked hay to the horses and poured alfalfa pellets for the lambs. As he crossed the yard to the tractor mower, a soccer ball bounced against his foot. Looking down, he picked it up and turned. Shelley and Anne stood in the front yard watching him.

"You kicked it too hard," Anne told Shelley before reaching her hands toward Scott. "Can we have the ball back?"

Hmm. Maybe this was a good time to be a father. The hay mowing could wait a few minutes.

He tossed the ball into the air above his head several times and caught it, testing its weight. Then he dropped it to the ground and trotted toward the girls, nudging the ball along with his booted feet.

"Who's the goalie?" he called as he reached the front lawn.

"I am," Shelley called. "Anne's teaching me how to be a good midfielder and make a goal. The flowerbox is the goal, but try not to trample Melanie's flowers."

He glanced at the colorful pansies, mentally warning himself to be careful. "I'll be a forward and help make a goal."

"Yay! Dad's gonna play," Shelley squealed. She then bent her knees, opened her arms wide and got serious. "I'm ready."

At first, Anne's mouth dropped open in surprise. Then a determined look covered her face. "If you're gonna play, you have to pass the ball sometimes. Soccer's a team sport."

"You got it." Scott chuckled, soft-kicking the ball over to her. He heard the screen door clap closed and saw Melanie out of his peripheral vision as she came down off the porch. It'd been years since he'd played ball as part of a family.

Anne passed the ball back to him. When he got close enough, he gave a short kick and popped the ball over to Melanie.

"I'm not playing." She laughed, nudging the ball with her toe.

"You are now. I'll be a defender on Shelley's team. You can help Anne score a goal." Scott moved over to help his daughter block the ball.

"Come on, Mom. Kick it." Anne ran forward and Melanie had no choice but to join the game.

Scott watched Melanie's expression as she pressed her tongue against her top lip. She sidled the ball along with her foot before passing it to Anne. The girl caught him off guard with her speed and he barely blocked the ball as it shot toward him.

"Nice kick," he told her before retrieving the ball from the driveway and bouncing it back to her. "Go again."

She maneuvered the ball expertly, passing it to her mother, then back again. Scott panted as he chased after them, trying to steal the ball back.

He came up behind Melanie, who whipped her head around and shrieked. "Oh, no, you don't."

The woman wasn't big, but she was agile and as fast as her daughter. She almost slipped past him, but her foot caught on his ankle and she tripped. He reached out to catch her, twisting his body to bear the brunt of the fall. They tumbled into the grass, laughing. He rolled, his arms around her as she lifted her head and smiled down into his eyes. The palms of her hands rested against his chest, her long hair spilling across his cheek, tickling his nose.

"Did I hurt you?" she asked.

He shook his head, unable to speak. He studied the oval slant of her beautiful green eyes, his heart pounding like a drum. She wore very little makeup, but she didn't need it. Her natural beauty more than made up for the enhancements that other women sought in a bottle or jar.

She blinked, her soft breath fanning

against his lips. Without warning, she hopped up, breaking the moment as she chased after the ball. Scott followed more slowly, his brain groggy. With a flick of her foot, Melanie arched the ball over to Anne who drew back her leg for a solid kick. Seeing it coming Shelley squealed with fear and scrunched her face, arms and legs together so she wouldn't get hit. The ball zipped past her and rolled into Melanie's pansies.

"Goal!" Anne lifted her arms in the air. "Shelley, you're supposed to block the ball, not hide from it."

"But it almost hit me."

"That's the idea, dummy. If it hits you, it won't score a goal."

"I'm not dumb."

Bravo! Scott liked Shelley to defend herself.

"Anne, no name-calling. Apologize right now," Melanie said.

Anne pursed her lips. "I'm sorry. You're not dumb. You just don't know how to play the game right. If you knock it away like this —" she showed the maneuver with her arms "— it won't go into the goal and it won't hurt because you'll have padding on."

Shelley nodded. "I'll try."

While Anne drew back and kicked the ball again, Scott brushed at the grass stains on the elbow of his shirt. His gaze kept moving to rest on Melanie. He couldn't keep his eyes off her as she chased after the ball.

This time, Shelley flung out her arms and stopped the ball. It wasn't a very graceful movement, but she'd tried.

"I did it! I did it!"

"Great job! Well done, honey." Scott opened up the floodgates of praise, taking advantage of this opportunity to build his child's confidence. He hugged Shelley, whirling her around on the lawn until she squealed with delight.

"Much better," Anne said.

Scott liked his daughter's willing attitude. He would never tell her that she was a bit of a wimp, but he was glad she tried so hard. The little girls were definitely good for each other.

They all gathered together at the front of the flower box, laughing and offering more suggestions to Shelley. Scott rested his hand on Anne's shoulder. "I didn't know you were such a good player. Shelley's got a good teacher."

At first, the girl smiled at his compliment. Then, as if remembering who he was, the smile slid from her mouth, replaced by a frown. She stepped away, withdrawing into herself.

Shutting him out.

Melanie must have noticed. "Okay, enough play for one evening. You girls have chores to do."

"Ahh, but I was just getting the hang of it." Shelley picked up the ball.

"We can practice again tomorrow. Come on." Anne took the ball and raced toward the lambing shed. Shelley followed close on her heels.

"That was fun." Scott smiled at Melanie, enjoying the domestic feeling that settled over him. Except for Anne's animosity, he felt as though he belonged here. As if they were a real family.

But not quite.

"Look at that sunset." She pointed toward the western mountains where the fading sun lit up the sky with red and orange clouds.

"Now that's a sunset."

They stood close together, their arms touching. In those tranquil moments with her, Scott felt more content than ever before in his life. He turned to face her, his fingers twining with hers.

"Melanie, I wish we could —"

She moved her hand away. "Don't say it, Scott. It'd only make things more difficult . . . for both of us." She brushed her fingers against her chin and took a step toward the door. "I'd better get back into the kitchen and check on my chicken. I don't want it to burn."

The magic bubble burst.

He shook his head, trying to clear his mind. What had he been about to say? He wasn't sure, but he knew she felt it, too. The attraction between them. Like a current of high-voltage electricity. "I'd better get out into the hay field."

"See you later." She waved.

"Yeah. Later."

Scott turned and headed toward the mower, wishing he could say something more intelligent. Wishing he dared ask Melanie out on a formal date. No doubt Anne wouldn't like that. And Melanie wouldn't feel comfortable with it, either. Too much censure stood between them. They were friends and nothing more. He had to keep reminding himself of that. But it was getting harder to remember.

Melanie stepped out on the back porch of her house and took a deep breath. The evening air smelled of freshly cut hay. Crickets chirped from the side of the house. Except for the drinks of water and lemonade she'd taken out to him, Scott hadn't stopped to take a break since he'd gone out to the fields. It was getting late and the girls should be in bed.

Scott must be worn out.

Taking a flashlight with her, she pushed her arms into the sleeves of her sweater and headed across the back lawn toward the south pasture. The sun had faded behind the western mountains, but she could see the headlight from the hay mower glistening at the end of the field. Scott had killed the motor ten minutes earlier and she hoped that meant he was finished with the mowing. She climbed over the fence and clicked on the flashlight as she walked the furrowed field.

Long windrows of freshly mowed hay led the way. With the use of her farm equipment, she was able to rake the drying hay and even bale and stack it, but mowing always gave her problems. If there was an equipment failure, it required pure muscle to fix it and she just wasn't strong enough. She owed Scott a lot for his help.

"Hi there," he called as she approached.

Careful not to shine the light in his eyes, she panned the beam of the flashlight over him. He knelt on the ground, working to replace a blade on the mower.

"Is there a problem?" she asked.

He flashed a wide smile, his left cheek

streaked with dirt. He'd removed his beat-up cowboy hat and she caught the gleam of his sweat-dampened hair. He'd worked hard tonight, winning her deep-seated gratitude.

"Nothing I can't handle. I just finished the mowing and thought I'd check the blades to make sure she's ready for tomorrow night."

His consideration pleased her. Knowing he'd be here again tomorrow evening brought her more relief than she could express. Being so short on funds, she dreaded having to hire someone else to bring in her hay. She owed Scott. A lot. She had to pay him somehow.

"I can't tell you how much I appreciate this." She stood nearby, shining the flashlight on his hands to help him see better. Using the front weight support of the tractor as an anvil, he struck the back edge of a broken blade with a heavy rock, knocking the damaged rivet out of the bar.

He didn't look up as he spoke. "Likewise I appreciate your looking after Shelley for me. She's happy for the first time since her mother left us. Anne even has her playing soccer. She refused to play with me whenever I offered, so I'm grateful that she's found a friend to talk her into it."

Her heart ached for him. How miserable both he and Shelley must have been to lose their wife and mother. Melanie still cried over losing Aaron, mourning what their life together might have been like if he hadn't started drinking.

If he hadn't gone up onto the mountain during a thunderstorm.

"I think I'm getting the better end of the bargain," she said. "You're saving me a lot by working on my ranch. I'd like to pay you some as well as tend Shelley for you."

He stood and dusted off his hands. In the shadows of the headlight, his gaze locked with hers. "That wasn't our agreement, Mrs. McAllister. I promised I'd work for you, and I meant it."

His kindness amazed her. She couldn't help smiling, thankful that this good man had come into her life. She'd realized at the ranchers' meeting that she'd misjudged him. She'd never met a more intelligent, self-assured and hardworking man. Being so near him sent shivers racing up her spine. Before she could stop herself, she stepped close and kissed his cheek. He smelled of freshly cut hay.

He stiffened and she drew back a bit too fast. What was she thinking, being so forward with him? When they'd shared the sunset together earlier, she'd stopped him from saying something they both might regret. She felt much too comfortable around this man. How she wished they could be more than friends. But the situation was impossible. And getting more difficult all the time.

"I . . . I just wanted to thank you for everything you've done." She folded her arms against the cool air and jutted her chin toward the house. "At least let me give you supper. You must be starved."

He chuckled. "That I am. I could eat a straw hat right now. Let me drive the mower back to the barn first."

Again, his thoughtfulness impressed her. He always worked neatly, even when he was hungry and tired. He never left equipment out or empty of gasoline, but always put everything back in good order so it was ready for the next usage.

She walked back to the house, then washed her hands. Using a hot pad, she took a heaping plate of fried chicken, mashed potatoes and gravy from the oven.

The girls sat at the table, scarfing down pieces of warm apple pie with ice cream.

"Is Daddy coming in now?" Shelley asked.

"Yep, he's just finished the mowing for tonight." Melanie opened the fridge and

203

retrieved the milk and butter along with a plate of homemade rolls.

Scott came in and doffed his boots. "Wow! Something smells good."

"It's ready. Get washed up."

He stepped into the laundry room. The spray of water sounded as he turned on the faucet. Melanie had put out a fresh towel for him. By the time he'd scrubbed the grime from his face and hands, she had his meal ready.

He sat down and smiled at Shelley and Anne. "How are my favorite girls tonight?"

"Fine," Shelley said. "I was getting worried. You took a long time working tonight."

"I'm fine, sweetheart. It had to be done." He bit into a piece of chicken and released a sigh of relish. "This is delicious."

"You're supposed to bless it first." Anne frowned.

Scott froze, his gaze darting over to Melanie. "I'm sorry. I didn't mean to be rude."

Melanie shook her head. "We've already blessed it. Go ahead and eat."

She shot a warning look at her daughter. Anne's mouth quirked with disapproval before she concentrated on her apple pie. Melanie picked up the dish towel and dried a plate. How she wished Anne could be more accepting of Scott. The girl was young, but she should understand how much they needed Scott's help around the ranch. He'd made such a difference for them. He wasn't like the other rangers who had come to town. Scott was different, in every way.

Scott continued eating hungrily. "Tomorrow, I think I can finish mowing the other fields. We'll have your hay put up in no time."

"In a few days, I can go out with the side rake and roll the hay so it'll dry better." Melanie leaned her hip against the counter, feeling content with Scott and their kids in her kitchen. She couldn't help wondering if this comfortable companionship was how it should be for all families as they talked and planned their lives. She'd never experienced this contentment with Aaron and couldn't help wishing she could always feel this way.

"Don't knock yourself out," he said. "I can turn the hay on Friday night, after I get off work." He glanced at Anne. "Could you pass me the butter, sugar?"

Anne dropped her fork and pushed back from the table so fast that her chair toppled over with a clatter. "Get it yourself. I'm not your sugar. And you're not my dad."

The girl raced from the room. The stunned silence was followed by the slamming of her bedroom door.

Scott's jaw fell slack as he looked at Melanie. "I'm sorry, Melanie. I didn't mean to upset her."

Shelley's eyes widened and her bottom lip quivered. "Why'd Anne talk to you like that, Dad? Is she okay?"

Melanie stepped over to the table and picked up the chair before pushing it under the table. "Anne's fine. I think I'd better go talk to her."

"Let me." Scott stood and rounded the table.

"I'm not so sure that's a good idea."

He rested his hand on Melanie's arm, his eyes filled with concern. "Until we become friends, she'll never trust me. I think it's time we talked. Don't worry . . . I'll be gentle. Why don't you listen in?"

"Okay." Melanie nodded and said a silent prayer.

As Scott walked down the hallway, Melanie followed, staying back so she could listen without being detected by her daughter. Scott gave her a reassuring smile as he knocked on Anne's door.

"Go away."

Undeterred, he turned the knob and entered the lion's den. Melanie peeked around the door and saw Anne sitting at her desk, coloring furiously.

"Anne, can I talk to you for a few minutes?" Scott said.

"No! Go away."

The mattress squeaked as he sat on the edge of the bunk bed. "I'll tell you what. You don't have to talk. Just listen to me for a moment."

Silence. But that was better than shouting. Even so, Melanie wasn't heartened by the lack of response.

Scott's voice filtered out into the hallway, soft and gentle. "I was a few years older than you when my father died. We ran a sheep ranch in Northern Nevada. When he died, I wasn't big or strong enough to really help my mom a lot and we had to sell our ranch before the bank foreclosed on us."

Anne gasped. "You did?"

Melanie closed her eyes at the emotion in her daughter's voice. This was her greatest fear right now. That they'd lose Opal Ranch. Frank Donaldson kept offering to buy her land for a pittance of what it was worth, but Melanie kept refusing to give up the fight. Until now, she hadn't realized that Anne was worried about it, too.

"Yep. And my mother died a year later. I had nobody in the world."

Anne made a derisive sound. "If you were

207

a rancher, why'd you become a ranger?"

Melanie caught the tone of disgust in her daughter's voice.

"I couldn't be a rancher anymore, no matter how much I wanted to," Scott said. "But I figured if I worked hard, I could work my way through school and learn to be a good ranger so I could help other ranchers."

"Really? That's why you did it?"

"Yep. Not all rangers are bad, just like not all ranchers are bad. I've learned that most people are basically good inside. Sometimes we just forget to be kind to one another. Fighting is easier. It takes more patience and self-control to get along."

"You mean like how the Donaldsons won't sell us groceries anymore?"

"I guess that's a good example. But it wouldn't be very nice if I pulled Mr. Donaldson's grazing permits, would it?"

"No. Mom said Jesus doesn't like mean tricks like that."

"That's true. I think right now, you're afraid," Scott continued. "You're worried you and your mom might lose Opal Ranch. Am I right?"

No sound came from the room, but Melanie knew it was true. Her daughter was frightened and insecure, just as she was.

"You don't need to worry," Scott said. "I'll

do everything in my power to help your mom keep your ranch safe."

"You mean it?" Hope filled the girl's voice, as if she couldn't quite believe what he'd said.

"It's my promise to you. Okay?"

Melanie couldn't resist peeking around the door. Her daughter shrugged, then nodded. "Okay, but once you make a promise, you have to keep it."

Scott patted the girl's shoulder. "I intend to. You can count on it."

Melanie's heart squeezed hard. Scott's words reached deep inside her, giving her hope. It wasn't just Anne who needed to hear his promise. It had been a long time since Melanie had the faith to believe in anyone other than God. Maybe Scott was the answer to her prayers. Maybe the Lord had sent him and Shelley to Snyderville to help out. And Scott didn't even know it.

CHAPTER TEN

Melanie awoke with a start. Alarm prickled her skin and she stared into the darkness above her bed, feeling disoriented. The nightlight by the bathroom door cast an eerie red glow down the hallway. Bob's barking mingled with yells and raucous laughter from outside the house.

"What on earth?" Who could be here at this time of night?

She glanced at the bedside clock, which read 1:37. As she jumped out of bed, she grabbed her bathrobe and thrust her arms into the sleeves.

Scurrying to the front room, Melanie drew back the curtains and peered outside. The headlights of two trucks almost blinded her and she jerked back, blinking. One truck skidded through her wide driveway, turning circles, flipping up gravel as the driver and passengers screamed with delight. Though she couldn't make out their faces in the shadows, two teenage boys tromped through her delphiniums before pelting her house with what appeared to be eggs. The crack and splat struck her picture window, followed by a sickening crash.

Gasping in fear, Melanie stepped to the side as shattered glass covered the cream-colored carpet. A rock rolled and landed by her bare feet.

Melanie cried out as a sliver of glass bit into her skin. Bob yelped in pain and she watched in horror as a boy pelted the dog with eggs. The dog growled and snapped, lunging for the boy until he gave up his torment. That's when Melanie got good and mad. Nobody attacked her dog and got away with it.

Hopping on her good foot, she brushed the glass away. Then she thrust her feet into her garden clogs sitting beside the door. As she passed through the kitchen, glass crunched beneath her feet. She reached for the cordless phone and dialed 9-1-1. While it rang, she went to the back room, turned on a desk lamp, entered the code into the gun safe, then removed Aaron's loaded rifle.

She had a right to defend her home.

The emergency operator came on the phone line and she quickly reported her address and the intrusion. When the operator asked for details, Melanie lost patience. "Just wake up Sheriff Chambers and tell him to get out to Opal Ranch fast."

She turned off the phone and tossed it onto the sofa before she cocked the rifle and returned to the front door.

"Momma!" Anne screamed as she came running down the hall, her eyes wide with fear.

"Stay back, sweetheart," Melanie ordered. "There's glass all over the floor. I want you to stay right there until I find out what's going on, okay?"

"Okay." Anne's voice quivered as she cowered beside the wall in her thin night-gown.

Anger flared anew as Melanie thought of her little girl being awakened in the middle of the night to a bunch of hooligans egging their house. She flipped on the porch light and the tall mercury vapor lights before she jerked open the front door. The lights bathed the yard in blue, but clearly outlined the five culprits. Two of the vandals were big and tall, their body size unmistakable. Melanie thought they must be Ryan and Luke Donaldson. Without being able to see their faces clearly, she couldn't be sure of their identities.

"Let's get outta here," a boy yelled.

Melanie stepped outside amid a mass retreat.

"Come on! Get in," one of the drivers called to his friends.

Lifting the rifle, Melanie fired into the air. The boys let out a screech of fear. Good! Maybe they'd think twice before causing trouble at Opal Ranch again.

Tires squealed, shooting up rocks. Boys jumped into the backs of the two trucks as their drivers sped toward the main road. Melanie squinted her eyes, studying the license plate number on one vehicle, repeating it over and over again so she wouldn't forget it.

She had them now. She was not about to stand for these shenanigans.

After the boys left, Melanie wrote down the license plate number and kept the rifle near as she went to comfort Anne. Sitting on the floor in the hallway, she held her trembling girl close.

"Wh-what did they want? Wi-will they come back?" Anne sobbed.

"Shh, no, sweetheart. I think they're gone. The police will be here soon. Don't cry now. Where's my big girl?"

Anne hiccupped and wiped her eyes. "I'm right here, Mom. But I didn't like that."

"Neither did I."

It took twenty minutes to calm Anne down. Then, Melanie turned on every light in the house and they both got dressed. Melanie stepped out on the back porch and whistled for Bob. The dog didn't come to her, but she didn't dare leave her house to go and look for the animal. She prayed that he was okay. They had gotten the sheepdog as a pup and Aaron had trained the animal. That had been in the early years of their marriage, before a bottle took precedence over everything else. Melanie sure wished Aaron were here right now, guarding and protecting them.

And then she thought about Scott Ennison. He would have taught those boys a lesson about terrorizing women and children in the middle of the night.

Anne retrieved the broom and dustpan to clean up the glass, but Melanie shook her head. "Not yet, sweetie. We need to wait for the sheriff. He'll want to see the evidence."

"What's this?" Anne picked up the rock and handed it to Melanie.

"That's the rock that broke our picture window. There's a note attached." A piece of white paper had been folded and attached with a rubber band. Melanie pulled the paper free and opened it. It read:

Stop tending the ranger's brat or you'll be sorry.

"What does it say?"

Melanie folded the paper and tucked it inside her pants pocket. "Nothing for you to worry about. Why don't you get us both a jacket from the coat closet? The night's a bit chilly."

Actually it was quite warm outside, but nerves and fear had made both her and Anne shake uncontrollably. Maybe a jacket would help.

Anne gave her mom a quizzical look, but did as she was asked. Melanie wanted to distract her daughter. It would do no good to frighten Anne even more by revealing the contents of the note.

It took the police forty minutes to arrive. Sitting in her living room with Anne cuddled close to her side, Melanie related everything that had happened that night. She handed the note and license plate number to Sheriff Chambers, the only law enforcement officer in Snyderville.

"The note was attached to the rock they threw through my window."

Sheriff Chambers scanned the message, looking stern. Thank goodness he was neither a rancher nor a ranger. He had a reputation for being honest and fair and she was counting on him to put a stop to what happened tonight. She never wanted a repeat performance.

She explained her identification of the two Donaldson boys.

"You're sure it was them?"

She shook her head. "I didn't see their faces clearly, but very few people around here are that size."

"The license plate number will tell us a lot. I'll look into it. I can accompany you into town if you'd like to stay there tonight."

"I'm not leaving my home. I doubt they'll come back. Not now that they know I have a rifle."

The sheriff glanced at Anne, seeming cautious of his words so he didn't further upset the girl. "This could have been very serious, if it had gotten out of hand."

"Yes," Melanie agreed. "Someone needs to pay for the damages to my home."

"With the description of the boys and the license plate number, it should be easy to track down the culprits. I'll see that they pay for what they've done. Do you want to press charges?"

Melanie hesitated, remembering what Aaron had said about bullies. If she let it go this time, it might be worse the next time.

She had to stand up to these bullies. "Yes."

"Fair enough."

He left and Melanie tucked Anne back into bed, then went to turn off the light.

"Don't leave me, Mom." The girl sat up, her eyes glimmering with panic.

"I won't leave. Never, ever will I let anyone hurt you." She lay beside Anne on the narrow bunk bed and held her until the girl fell asleep. She pulled the covers up over Anne's shoulders and watched her for several minutes, adoring the girl with her eyes. How she loved Anne. How heartbroken she would be if anything bad happened to her little girl.

At times, Melanie felt so helpless. So alone.

She went outside to peruse the damage to her house. Her flowers were all but ruined. Egg goo and shells splotched the front of her house and porch. In the morning, she'd take pictures of the damage before using the garden hose to squirt off the mess. She might need to repaint the house.

Gazing at the long road to make sure that no headlights were in view, she then walked out to the barn to find Bob. She turned on the light and found the old dog huddled back in the stall with Wilma, the gentle mare Shelley always rode whenever she came to the ranch.

"There you are," Melanie spoke with relief. "Hey, boy. It's okay, they're gone."

She approached slowly and knelt beside the dog, searching him for injuries and grateful when she found that he was okay. He panted and wagged his bobbed tail, rubbing his graying head against her side.

"Yes, I'm glad to see you, too."

Over the years, she'd watched this brave dog face off wild coyotes, but now he was old. She hated that someone had hurt him just because she'd become friends with Scott Ennison. "I think you're gonna need a bath to get all the egg out of your fur, but you'll be fine. Why don't you come up to the house with me and I'll let you stay in Anne's room? I think you'd both feel better if you were together."

The dog licked her face and that's when Melanie lost it. Her proud courage left her in one, swift breath. Tears flooded her eyes and she wept. Now that the danger was past, she realized how frightened she'd been. And lonely. She was tired of being strong. Tired of the constant vigil she must maintain in order to put food on the table and ensure they paid the mortgage. Now she feared going to sleep. Feared those boys might return, hurt her family and destroy her home.

Please, God. Please help me carry these burdens. Help us stay safe.

If only Scott were here. He'd know what to do. It was easy to plague a lone woman and her child, but it was a totally different matter with a man on the scene. She couldn't imagine those vandals standing up to Scott Ennison. He seemed to control every situation. Not with rage and a booming voice, but with calm assurance and a strong personality.

She remembered his soothing voice as he freed the deer from the barbed-wire fence and how he had spoken with compassion to Anne. He'd worked so hard here at Opal Ranch and kept his promises to her and the other ranchers.

How she wished he —

No! It did no good to wish for something that could never be. Not now. Not ever.

"That does it. I'm going to find someone else to look after Shelley for me." Scott stood on the front porch of Melanie's home.

Jets of water shot from the pistol nozzle on the hose as she sprayed dried egg off the house.

"No, you're not." She didn't look at him, but her delicate jaw locked with stubbornness. "I won't have people telling me who I can and cannot have here in my home. I want Shelley to stay right here. I'll go bankrupt first before I ever sell my ranch to the Donaldsons."

Guilt rested on Scott's shoulders like a giant sledge. This had happened because of him. He had no right to endanger Melanie and Anne because he was the forest ranger.

"Think about Anne. Think about your own safety," he said.

Thankfully the two girls had gone to the barn to feed the lambs and weren't here to listen to this conversation. He figured he and Melanie could handle this situation, but their little girls were innocent and deserved to live free of fear.

Melanie tossed the hose aside and reached for a bucket of hot, soapy water. Using a sponge, she scrubbed furiously at a stubborn splotch of egg yolk. Still, she didn't look at him, speaking as she worked. "I *am* thinking of Anne. They egged your house and frightened Shelley, too. If we separate our daughters now, it'll mean they've won. At least right now, the girls have each other to depend on. If you take Shelley away, our girls will have no one."

Her reasoning was sound. When he'd been awakened in the middle of the night to find his house being egged, he'd never considered that the culprits might also have vandalized Melanie's house. At least the vandals had run off before breaking any of his windows. This time, no serious harm had been done. But what if the thugs got braver and caught Melanie or one of the girls alone? What if they hurt one of them . . . ?

He stepped close and took hold of Melanie's wet hand, forcing her to face him. Her angry eyes met his and he felt lost. His head pounded with fear. For her.

He loved her. The realization came slowly and with such force that it felt like a physical blow. He loved her and Anne and Opal Ranch. He had to keep them safe. "I can't always be there to protect you, Mel. If anything happened to you or our girls, I don't think I could —"

His throat closed. He'd almost blurted out how much he cared. How much he wished they could be a real family. For so long, he'd refused to even think about his feelings for Melanie. Thinking about it and saying it out loud would make it real. And he could have no future with the McAllisters. Not like this.

They stood together, gazing into each other's eyes. Suspended in time. Then Melanie broke down, sobbing against his chest, the soggy sponge dropping free of her fingers and landing on the porch with a splat. He held her for several minutes, breathing her in, wishing he could ease her pain. Wishing he could handle this situation better than he'd done.

Wishing she were his.

"I'm sorry, Scott." She drew away and wiped her nose with the sleeve of her shirt. "I don't know what's come over me. I guess it's just nerves."

His arms ached to hold her again. To comfort her. To tell her he'd take care of her and Anne and everything would be just fine. "It's best if I take Shelley away."

"And where will you take her?"

He didn't know. He'd called Allison earlier this morning, but she'd hung up on him when he suggested that she should take Shelley for the summer, just until he could defuse some of the ranchers' animosity.

He had an old aunt who lived in Arizona, but he doubted that the elderly lady would be willing or able to take care of Shelley. His only alternative was to quit his job. And then how would he earn a living? In this economy, an out-of-work forest ranger might have a tough time. Quitting went against every instinct in his body. Losing his parents and the ranch at such an early age had ingrained a stubborn determination deep within him. Walking away from his job might destroy him, but at least it would keep Melanie and their girls safe.

Their girls. Funny how he couldn't think of them as separate anymore. They seemed to be part of one family, and yet they weren't.

But they should be.

He longed to take his relationship with Melanie to a higher level, but feared that he would only cause her more problems with the local ranchers. He had no right to step into the role of husband and father with the McAllisters. Look at how much misery he'd brought them just by being friends. If he and Melanie became romantically involved, it could prove disastrous.

"Please don't take Shelley anywhere else." Melanie's voice cracked and so did his heart. "Sheriff Chambers ran the license plate number and found it belonged to Frank Donaldson. The sheriff is dealing with the situation. Let's just all get back to normal and move on."

Normal? He wondered if that was even possible now.

"Okay," he agreed against his better judgment. "But as soon as we can, we're driving into Evanston and I'm getting you a satellite phone. I want you to be able to reach me no matter what time of day, no matter where you are."

"No, Scott. I can't accept that —"

He held up a hand and locked his jaw. "You're caring for my daughter, Melanie. I insist that you accept the phone. I'll feel better if you can reach me at all times."

She didn't argue and he breathed a sigh of relief.

She stood watching him as he climbed into his truck and drove back to town. Looking in his rearview mirror, he saw her pick up the bucket to continue her cleaning. She was a compassionate, strong and independent woman, but she wasn't invincible. The thought of someone hurting her made his insides clench. He wished he could stay with her all day, just to make sure she and their girls were safe. He loved working at Opal Ranch. Loved being part of the McAllisters' life.

Maybe it was time he asked God for help one more time.

"Kick the ball, Shelley. Kick it!" Anne yelled at the other girl as they raced down the soccer field at the only elementary school in town.

Melanie watched from the sidelines, cheering the girls on. Nina Donaldson sat on the opposite side of the field. Melanie thought about approaching the woman to talk about what her sons had done, but decided to let the sheriff handle it instead. Then Melanie wouldn't be tempted to say things she might regret later on.

Shelley and Anne looked so cute in their red-and-white uniforms and knee-high socks. When they'd driven into town for practice, Anne had explained the rules of the game in great detail. Although she was timid about stealing the ball, Shelley was fast and she raced ahead, even surpassing the boys in an attempt to make a goal. She had her father's natural grace. Now if she could just overcome her apprehension and get more aggressive.

Drawing back her leg, Shelley prepared to kick the ball. Bart Donaldson came out of nowhere, ramming her with his shoulder and knocking her down hard.

Melanie gasped and came up from her seat on the bleachers. Coach Allen blew the whistle and the game stopped. The players milled around.

"Get out of the way, Smelly Shelley." Bart smirked as he strolled away, but Shelley didn't get up. She lay in the grass, her shoulders quivering as she cried softly.

Melanie hopped down from the bleachers and raced onto the field, followed by other parents, including Nina Donaldson.

"Shelley, are you okay?" Melanie knelt over the girl, who lay clutching her left knee to her chest. She grimaced in pain and gasped for breath.

"It's her leg," someone said.

"Is she okay?" another person asked.

"You did that on purpose." Anne pushed Bart, her face looking fierce as she held up her fists, ready for a fight.

"I was just trying to get the ball away," Bart claimed in an innocent tone.

"No, you weren't. You tried to hurt Shelley on purpose."

"Stop fighting," Coach Allen ordered.

Melanie glanced up and saw Nina step near, placing her large frame between Anne and her son.

"I . . . I'm okay. It just hurts." Shelley panted.

"Just lay still for a few minutes." Melanie caressed the girl's face and pressed her hand against her shoulder, giving Shelley a few moments to let the pain subside. She hoped the injury wasn't serious. She could just imagine explaining to Scott why she had to make another emergency trip to the hospital in Evanston.

When Shelley sat up, Melanie exhaled an anxious breath. The girl finally stood with help and tested her leg gingerly. She could stand, but the knee looked swollen.

Anne glared at Bart. "Don't you dare touch her ever again."

The boy jutted his jaw. "And what if I do? What are you gonna do about it, ranger lover?"

"I'll make you very sorry."

"She's an outsider. She doesn't belong here," Bart spat.

"She does, too. She's a better runner than you are."

"Is not."

"Stop it, you two," Melanie said.

"Bart, that was a big foul." Coach Allen gripped the whistle hanging on a lanyard around his neck. "If we were in a real game, you would have been benched for that. You'll have to sit on the sidelines for the rest of practice."

"But I want to play," Bart whined.

"Then don't do that again." Coach turned his attention back to Shelley.

The boy sulked and griped to his mother. "Mom! I want to play. I don't have to sit out, do I?"

"You sit out or you leave the field. Your choice." Coach stood and faced Bart and his mother.

Nina lifted her chin higher in the air and she seemed to size up the coach before speaking. She could cause trouble for the coach, but that would do no good. No one else had volunteered to coach the team and Melanie doubted Nina would like to take over the job.

"Go sit down, Bart," Nina said.

"Ahh!" the boy groused as he stomped over to the bleachers and plopped down.

Bravo! At least someone stood up to the kid.

"What Bart did was uncalled for," Melanie told Nina.

Melanie had put up with too much of Aaron's foul temper to let this pass without comment. She couldn't believe Bart's mother didn't reprimand him. Didn't the woman realize her silence only encouraged her son to bully other people?

She longed to tell Nina exactly what she thought of her. In light of the fact that her two eldest sons had vandalized her house last week, Melanie had difficulty biting her tongue.

"It wasn't a foul," Nina exclaimed. "He was just protecting the goalie."

Coach shook his head. "It was a foul, Nina. Okay, kids, let's get back to practice."

Anne glared at Bart, her brown eyes spitting flame. Melanie feared that her daughter might attack the boy at any moment.

"Anne, leave it alone. Coach has taken care of it," Melanie said.

The girl jogged over to join the coach, but she didn't look happy. Heaven help Bart Donaldson if he ever hurt Shelley again. That thought brought a smile to Melanie's lips. She liked the way Shelley and Anne stuck up for one another.

Melanie focused on Shelley, helping the girl limp off the field. She'd speak with her daughter later on about this matter. Right now, she understood her child's animosity toward Bart and his family. They were all fast becoming enemies and Melanie didn't like it.

"Have you got her?" Coach asked, his hand resting on Shelley's arm.

Melanie nodded. "I'll take care of her."

"Good. Okay, clear the field." Coach blew his whistle and the parents returned to the sidelines.

Melanie sat Shelley on the bleachers, then knelt in front of her to examine her leg. "Where were you injured, sweetheart?"

"My knee."

Melanie pressed the injured area gently with her fingers. "I think it's a little swollen, but not too bad. Does it still hurt?"

Shelley shook her head and smiled. "Nope, it's okay now. Anne said I was bound to get hurt sometime. She said soccer's a rough sport, but if I'm tough, I can take it. I want to be strong like Anne."

"We'll get you an ice pack when we get home. You're so brave." Melanie patted the girl's cheek, feeling a strong maternal bond toward her. She never thought she could adore another child as much as she did her own, but she realized she'd protect Shelley at all costs. The girls were more than friends. They were more like —

Sisters.

Practice resumed, but Melanie knew the matter was anything but resolved. Now that Shelley was okay, she stepped over to chat with Nina Donaldson. Words boiled around in her mind, but she tried to remember what the Savior would do. She wondered if the Golden Rule applied when children were concerned. Right now, Melanie wanted to knock Nina Donaldson in the head.

As she approached, Nina glared at Melanie as if she was a bug under a microscope. "What do you want?"

"Don't you think this has gone far enough, Nina? What if Bart had broken Shelley's leg or hurt her seriously?"

"I don't know what you mean. My boy was just playing soccer."

Melanie rested one hand on her hip. "It looked more like tackle football to me."

"If the ranger's daughter can't handle the game, she should quit."

"This isn't about handling the game. Shelley just made the past two goals. She's good. But what Bart did was just mean."

"If you weren't so tied up with the forest ranger, you might feel differently. You used to be one of us."

One of us? Good heavens!

"Do you know how silly you sound? This isn't an us-against-them situation. These are children playing a simple game of soccer, Nina. I've never egged your house or thrown rocks through your windows. How would you feel if I came in the middle of the night to terrorize you and your family?"

Nina stared at her. "You'd better not. There's just you and that little girl against my husband and sons."

Melanie couldn't believe what she heard. "What is that supposed to mean? Are you so filled with hate that you would deliberately hurt my daughter and me? You who likes to make donations to the church and claims to be so religious?" Melanie pointed a finger at her. "Maybe you should take a hard look in the mirror and really ask yourself what you and your family have become."

The woman drew herself up to her full six feet and looked down her nose at Melanie. "At least I'm not a ranger lover."

Something snapped inside of Melanie. "They're children, Nina. What do they have to do with grazing allotments? It's not fair to torture the children over adult issues."

Nina brushed her off. "Why don't you go over there to the other side of the field? It's bad enough that you pressed charges against my sons. Now they'll have a police record."

"And that's supposed to be my fault? Believe me, I didn't ask them to vandalize my home."

"It was just a kids' prank. No real harm was done."

Melanie's head was reeling with anger, but she clamped an iron will on her emotions and spoke calmly and rationally. "A prank? Your older boys are grown men and should be protecting my little girl, not terrorizing her in the middle of the night. You're lucky Aaron wasn't there."

She let that statement speak for itself. Aaron had a foul enough temper that he might have shot one of the boys first and asked questions later.

"Aaron was a drunk. He couldn't even stand up straight."

"Yes, he was a drunk. But at least you still have your husband. Mine's gone." Bitterness filled Melanie's voice. And deep, soul-wrenching hurt.

For the first time since Melanie had known her, Nina's eyes filled with shame and she looked away. But she didn't apologize. She didn't say one word.

Melanie gnashed her teeth, longing to say a few more choice words no good Christian woman should ever utter. Instead, she turned and walked away, fuming inside. She had tried to reason with Nina. Tried to behave as the Savior would have her do, but realized her efforts were futile. Nina was filled with so much hate that she couldn't hear anything but anger.

Sometimes it was very difficult to love your enemy.

CHAPTER ELEVEN

He didn't want to be here. Driving through town, Scott pulled off to the side of the road and parked in the dirt near the community center. Emotions waged a war inside him as he looked at Shelley. The girl crinkled her nose, her eyes filled with resignation.

"I guess we have to do this," she said. "Anne told me it's what communities do. They help clean up the town."

She rubbed the elastic bandage he'd wrapped around her knee that morning. Melanie had told him what happened at soccer practice. Scott had paid a rather stilted visit to Frank Donaldson. Needless to say, it hadn't gone much better than Melanie's chat with Nina.

After cleaning the egg off their house, neither he nor Shelley wanted to help clean up trash along the outskirts of town. But they'd do it, because they wanted to be part of this community.

"We won't stay long. I don't want you walking on that knee very much." The promise was for her as well as himself. When they'd first come to Snyderville, he'd felt so certain he could make a difference here. The community cleanup was a great idea, but Scott couldn't help feeling angry at many of these people after all they'd put him and Shelley through.

Most of Scott's work and personal problems stemmed from the Donaldsons. He had to figure out a way to get Frank and his family to leave him and Shelley alone. But how? Scott had tried to be as considerate as possible. He'd made good on his promises, working as hard as he could.

They didn't need to be friends, but vandalism and bodily harm were not acceptable. If not for Melanie's encouragement, he might have given up and left town. He didn't want to expose his child to so much hatred. When he came to town, he didn't care what these people thought of him. That had changed somehow. He now cared about these people, and Melanie and Anne. And that bothered him. Intensely.

Caring meant he could be hurt again.

He stared out the windshield. People walked along the sides of the road, picking up old cans, paper and other trash.

We don't need to help these people! They don't want us here, so why keep trying? He wanted to say the words out loud, but didn't. What kind of message would that send to Shelley? Life wasn't easy here in Snyderville, but if he backed down, turned tail and hid out, he'd be sending his daughter a message that she could quit whenever life got difficult. Right now, he was fighting for his career, but he was also trying to teach his child an important lesson. She'd been a meek child when they first came to this town. Now he admired her spunk and courage.

Reaching across the seat, he pulled Shelley close for a quick hug. Normally she pushed him away, but this time, she clung to his arms. Hurt and defenseless.

He rested his chin on her hair, enjoying the sweet smell of her strawberry shampoo. "Don't be frightened, hon. I won't let anyone hurt you again."

"You can't stop Bart from knocking me down during soccer practice," she said.

He hated that she was right. He longed to protect her every minute of every day, but knew that wasn't possible.

"I thought you weren't going to play soccer anymore." Half of him wished she'd quit and the other half wished she'd dig in her heels and stubbornly continue to play, just to show Bart that he couldn't frighten her off.

She pulled away and smiled, rubbing his bristly chin. Her touch spoke volumes. There'd been a time in their lives not too long ago when she wouldn't come near him because she missed her mom. Since they'd moved to Snyderville, they'd drawn closer, depending on one another. At least one good thing had come out of his new assignment in this town.

And he'd met Melanie McAllister.

"I wasn't gonna play anymore, but Anne said when you get bucked off, you have to get back on the horse and ride again. I can't let Bart think I'm afraid of him or he'll just be meaner the next time. I have to show him that he can't hurt me."

How wise. Scott felt the same way about God. Scott had been deeply hurt when his wife left him and he'd turned to the Lord for comfort. When he didn't find it, he'd abandoned prayer. Scott had been bucked off hard, but now he didn't feel quite as angry anymore. Maybe it was time to dust himself off and renew his relationship with his Heavenly Father.

"Dad . . ." Shelley's voice trailed off as she contemplated her hands.

"Yes?"

"Don't tell Anne, but I'm afraid of Bart. He's lots bigger than me and he can be mean. He hates me."

How could an eleven-year-old boy hate this sweet little girl? What did these children know about love and hate? Parents needed to be careful how they spoke and acted around their children. They passed along their biases and opinions to their kids.

Scott squeezed her shoulder and smiled. "I don't think Bart hates you. He just hasn't gotten to know you yet. You'll just have to outrun him so he can't catch you."

She giggled. "That's easy. I can outrun all the other kids."

"Then score a lot of goals for your team, hon. And from now on, I'm going to arrange my schedule so I can be at your soccer practices. Bart won't bother you with me standing there watching — I can guarantee that."

"It's okay, Dad. Melanie protects me. You should have heard her tell Mrs. Donaldson off after Bart knocked me down. And Coach benched Bart for hitting me so hard. Bart didn't get to play for the rest of the day."

Thank goodness for Melanie and Coach Allen.

"I'm proud of you, Shelley. You're so

grown-up. I'm glad I have you with me."
He kissed her forehead.

"I love you, Daddy."

His heart constricted. How he loved hearing these words from his girl. "I love you too, pumpkin."

They got out of the truck and Scott reached into the back for their gloves, rakes and plastic bags. Normally he would have taken this opportunity to mingle with the townsfolk, to chat and become friendlier. But today he just didn't feel like it. He wanted to spend time with Shelley.

When he saw Melanie, he approached her from behind, his heart pounding within his chest. He couldn't figure out why her nearness twisted him inside out.

Using a long metal bar, she tried to pry a large rock free from the path edging the road. Only this woman would endeavor such a task. Although she wasn't big or strong, nothing seemed to get in her way when she had a task to tackle. She did what she had to do.

"Hey! There's Shelley." Anne pointed and Melanie stood straight and looked over her shoulder before wiping her face with her forearm.

"Hi! You got a problem there?" Scott asked as the girls greeted each other.

Melanie panted to catch her breath and tapped the rock with the toe of her tennis shoe. "It won't budge. Think you can get it to move?"

He jerked on his gloves and took the bar from her hands. "I can try."

He thrust the bar hard against the side of the rock before bracing it against the dirt for leverage. With one hard shove, the rock gave way. Scott bent over and pushed the rock. It rolled out of the way into the sagebrush.

Melanie laughed, her eyes sparkling in the sunlight. "Impressive. Now people won't trip over it when they walk by."

"I just hope my road repair project goes as well." He leaned on the bar, resting his gloved hands on the top point. She stepped closer and he gazed into her eyes, lost in pools of emerald green.

"I heard you're closing Deer Creek Road for five days while you replace the bridge over the creek."

"Yeah, the steep rock cliffs prohibit construction of a detour, so we'll have to close the road. It'll be worth it once the bridge is completed."

"Is that why you don't have the pipeline finished yet?"

Scott drew back and found Frank Donaldson standing behind him. For such a big man, Frank moved on cat's feet. That or Scott had been too occupied with Melanie to notice the other man.

"Hi, Frank. You here for the cleanup?" Scott looked for the man's tools, but saw none.

Frank's slitted eyes glimmered with distaste. "I'd like to clean out the ranger trash if I could."

Scott refused to be baited by the man or give in to his insults. He cocked his head and put a hand to one ear. "What's that? I didn't hear you."

Frank mumbled a sullen reply before speaking louder. "Why isn't the pipeline finished yet?"

"It just so happens that we ran into a problem several days ago. Over the night, a brown bear got into the pipe we had sitting beside the trench and chewed it up. So we've ordered more pipe. The project will take us an additional week to complete."

"I knew it," Frank crowed. "I knew you wouldn't keep your word."

Scott tensed, unable to believe this accusation. "I've kept my word, Frank. The pipe will be one week late."

"That's reasonable under the circumstances." Pete Longley stood several feet

241

away, shoving old newspaper into a plastic bag.

"How would you know?" Frank said. "You're a sheep man."

Caleb Hinkle paused in his work and leaned on the handle of his rake. "Well, I'm a cattle man, and I'm mighty grateful the water line's almost finished. Mr. Ennison's done a good job for us."

"You said you'd have the line finished in four weeks. Now it's taking five weeks," Frank said.

The nerve of that man! After years of waiting for the Forest Service to act, the ranchers were finally about to get their water line. Through no fault of Scott's, the project had been delayed one week. All the digging was finished, the cement slab had dried and the water trough had been installed.

Scott shook his head. "No matter what we do, you'll find some reason to complain. You're being unreasonable, looking for a fight where there isn't one."

Caleb pushed his hat back and wiped his damp brow. "What's gotten into you, Frank? We're lucky to finally have a good ranger here in Snyderville. You've got a bad temper for no reason."

Melanie folded her arms, her mouth quirked with disgust. "You used to be different, Frank. Ever since Thad died, you've been meaner than a grizzly and taking it out on anyone who crosses your path."

Frank's face darkened and he clenched his burly hands. He took a step closer to Melanie and Scott automatically stepped in front of her. He'd protect her to the death. Frank looked mad enough to beat her to a pulp and Scott wouldn't allow him to touch her. Not ever.

"You don't know what you're talking about, Melanie," Frank's voice rumbled deep in his chest. "This has nothing to do with my son dying."

"Doesn't it?" She moved around Scott, standing close by his side. "We've all lost people we love, but we have no right to take our grief out on others. Think about how your actions have impacted your wife and your other sons. They used to be happy, smiling and laughing. Now they sneak around town getting into trouble all the time. And it's mostly due to your bad attitude."

Scott flinched, wishing she'd bite her tongue. Her candor seemed to hit hard as Frank's face turned an ugly shade of beet red. Scott hadn't known Frank had lost a son and he wondered how it had happened. He'd ask Melanie later on. Right now,

243

antagonizing Frank wouldn't do them any good.

"Just get the pipeline finished." Frank glared at them for several pounding moments, his big hands clenched so hard that his knuckles whitened.

"It'll be done in one more week." Scott didn't realize he'd been holding his breath until Frank backed off and stomped away.

Caleb clapped his hand once on Scott's back. "I don't care what Donaldson says. I'm glad you're here."

"Me, too. You've proven yourself and you're welcome here." Tom Kinsey showed a sunburned grin.

"Thanks." Scott had never expected this kind of support. Although there were ranchers who still hated him, he also had friends here. Knowing that lightened his heart, as nothing else could.

When they had a moment alone, Scott looked at Melanie. "Do you have a death wish, young lady?"

She shook her head, her expression sad as she watched Frank's retreating back. "No, but someone had to say it. The entire town's been taking the brunt of Frank's rage for five years now. It's time someone called him on it."

"What happened to his son?"

She bent over and scooped up more dead leaves before stuffing them into a black plastic bag. "A truck accident. Frank was driving home from Evanston late one night and hit a deer. Thad was twenty-two years old at the time and had just graduated from the University of Wyoming. He wasn't wearing a seat belt and was killed instantly. Frank won't admit it, but I think he blames himself. He used to be a gruff, but nice, man. That all changed after Thad died. Frank hasn't stepped inside a church ever since and he became hateful to everyone."

Then Scott and Frank had something in common. Scott blamed himself for his divorce. Guilt weighed heavily on Scott's mind and he'd turned his back on the Lord. Seeing what had become of Frank, Scott realized that he didn't want to end up like the other man. Angry and unforgiving. Taking his rage out on everyone around him.

Knowing about Thad Donaldson's death gave Scott some insight into why Frank acted the way he did. Maybe Scott could cut the man some slack. But he still wouldn't tolerate Frank's sons vandalizing his house or threatening his girls.

His girls. That's how Scott thought of Melanie and their two daughters. Somewhere along the line, Scott had fallen in love with them. Because he loved them, he'd assumed responsibility for them. Even with the troubles they faced, Scott considered them his. Even Anne, who had been so hurt when she lost her father. Both the girls needed a daddy and a mommy to love them. Someone to look up to and trust. Whether Melanie admitted it or not, she and Anne needed him, just as he and Shelley needed them.

Now what? He longed to tell Melanie how he felt, but he didn't dare. His profession stood between them like a great steel wall. How could he make things work between them? He didn't think he could stand to be hurt again.

"Take it back!" Shelley yelled at Anne.

Scott turned. The two girls stood at the bottom of the ditch bank where they'd been raking weeds and garbage. From the angry glares on the girls' faces, Scott realized that they were fighting.

Great . . . that's all they needed right now.

"No, I won't. It's true," Anne hollered back.

"Then you're not my friend anymore."

"That's fine with me." Anne shoved the other girl. Shelley staggered on her injured leg, lost her balance and landed on her bottom in the tall weeds.

"Anne!" Melanie jumped across the ditch and went to help Shelley up. Scott was right behind her.

"You okay?" Scott asked Shelley.

The girl rubbed her knee, glaring at Anne.

Anne stomped off, heading down the road as fast as her legs would carry her.

"Anne!" Melanie called, but the girl kept going.

"What was that all about?" Scott asked his daughter.

Shelley glowered at the other girl. "She said you're still a rotten forest ranger. Once a rotten forest ranger, always a rotten forest ranger. So I called her a rotten rancher."

Melanie clenched her eyes closed and let out a hissing breath. She clearly shared his exasperation over this contentious situation.

Truth be told, Scott was growing incredibly weary of this battle. It was one thing to have the town hate him and his job, but he was at a loss as to how to resolve the problem with these girls. "I thought you two had stopped your fighting."

Tears beaded in the corners of Shelley's eyes. "You're the only thing we ever fight about, Dad. I'm a ranger's daughter and Anne's a rancher. It'll always be that way."

"Calling each other names won't solve anything. You two should be friends, not enemies." Scott said the words automatically, conscious of Melanie standing beside him listening.

"She started it," Shelley said.

"I don't care. You finish it. What about you two being half dogies? I thought that was more important than being rangers or ranchers."

"Anne doesn't think so. She doesn't like you, Dad. And if she doesn't like you, then I don't like her." Shelley limped over to pick up her plastic bag.

Scott inhaled a sharp breath, feeling as though he'd been slugged in the gut. Anne hated him. In spite of everything he'd tried to do to win her trust. He could forget about telling Melanie how he felt about her.

"I think it's time I took Shelley home. I'm worried about her leg." From Melanie's sympathetic expression, Scott knew she didn't buy his excuse.

"I'm sorry, Scott. For everything," she said.

"Yeah, me, too."

"I'll speak to Anne again."

"No." He shook his head. "I made her a promise and I need to prove myself to her, Mel. It'll take time."

But how much time? What could he do to prove himself to Anne and win her trust?

Until he did, he couldn't make her and Melanie part of his family. And he wanted them for keeps.

By Friday evening, Scott looked forward to a free evening. He'd worked hard to coordinate the various projects he had going for the ranchers. Thankfully, the work crew had completed the pipeline up on Three Creek. Frank should be pleased. For once.

Last night, Scott had finished baling Melanie's hay, which was now safe in the stack yard at Opal Ranch. To celebrate, Melanie had invited Scott and Shelley over to her house for dinner, a movie and popcorn. One more hour of work and he could go see his girls . . . and have another opportunity to win Anne over. And yet a dark cloud of reservation hung over him.

His girls. Melanie, Anne and Shelley. They'd become his whole world. If only he could make them all his.

The phone rang in the outer office and Karen's urgent voice filtered through the open door. Scott almost groaned out loud. Now what?

As predicted, Karen appeared in his doorway moments later, reaching across his desk to hand him a piece of paper. "Looks like we've got a wildfire. Owen Thompson was out on Rattlesnake Mountain today. On his way home, he saw some boys parked off the main road, drinking beer. They had a campfire in Simpson's Meadow. Terry Hansen just called to report that she was out riding her horse and saw a lot of smoke coming from that vicinity."

"Did Owen Thompson recognize the boys?"

"He said no, but something in his voice led me to believe that he knows more than he's saying."

Which meant he knew their identities, but didn't want to get them into trouble.

Great! Another manmade forest fire. "Hopefully it's nothing. I'll drive over and check it out now. Stay close to the radio and I'll report what I find."

He pushed back from his desk and reached for his ranger hat hanging on the wall. Due to such a wet winter, fire season had remained relatively quiet this summer. In early June, Simpson's Meadow was filled with verdant green grass and sedges. By mid-August, the meadow had turned to dry kindling. All it needed was a lit match to set it off. Ideal conditions for a nasty brush fire.

Scott drove his light green Forest Service truck outside of town, heading for Simpson's Meadow. He fought the anxious urge to speed. It would take twenty minutes to reach the meadow and he had a bad feeling about this.

Fifteen minutes later, plumes of black smoke rose in the northern sky. Definitely a fire with lots of fuel.

A car and truck had pulled off the side of the road. Two men, a woman and several kids stood in the dirt talking, gesturing at the smoke and snapping pictures of the fire. Just what he needed right now. Tourists gawking at a range fire.

Taking out his binoculars case, Scott joined them. One of the men was none other than Marty Taylor.

"Boy, am I glad to see you! I just called your office on my cell phone," Marty said.

Scott bit off a grouchy retort. Now that the ranchers needed the Forest Service, they were glad to see him. Scott tried to feel charitable, but the past attack on his home and daughter — not to mention the Mc-Allisters — left him feeling irritable.

"Did any of you see some boys around here with a campfire?" he asked.

They all shook their heads. Which meant that unless Owen Thompson was willing to disclose the identities of the kids, they might never find out who had started the blaze.

Smoke burned Scott's eyes. He wasn't

surprised to find Marty here. The fire was close to his ranch. To get to the Taylor and Donaldson ranches, the fire would first have to go through Opal Ranch. Currently the wind was blowing west toward the mountains. Away from Opal Ranch.

Scott removed the binoculars from their carrying case and held them up to look through. Smoke choked the sky with red flames dancing beneath, moving fast.

"Is it serious?" a man hovering beside him asked.

"Any wildfire is serious."

With plenty of fuel and wind, the flames fanned across the dry meadow, consuming everything in its path. Heading toward the phone lines.

A sense of urgency built within Scott. He had to warn Melanie. Every person he cared about was at Opal Ranch.

Scott reached for his radio. "Ennison to Karen."

A brief pause of static.

"This is Karen. Go ahead." Karen's voice scratched out of the radio.

"We've got a brush fire in Simpson's Meadow, about fifty acres. At current wind speed, it'll be over 125 acres in an hour. It's currently on private property, burning toward forest land. Acknowledge."

"Affirmative."

"Can you reach the McAllisters and the Donaldsons to warn them?"

"I've already tried, but when I called the McAllisters, I got no answer."

Scott had to assume the phone lines were down. He didn't need to worry yet. The fire was burning away from Opal Ranch. He had time to warn Melanie. Right now, he had a responsibility to control this fire.

"Karen, get hold of Jim. Tell him we have an incident here. We need a crew to build fire line as soon as possible. The wind's picking up."

Static squawked on the radio.

"Affirmative. I've already put Jim on standby. We'll have two pumper trucks to you within sixty minutes."

"You're the best. And can you call the phone company? We've got phone lines edging the meadow. I think the fire's reached them already. That might be why you can't reach the McAllisters."

"I'll call the phone company."

"Good. And I'll radio the Bureau of Land Management and the Supervisor's Office right now."

"Roger that. Be careful out there."

"Will do. Out." Scott signed off, then radioed the BLM and the Supervisor's Office to make them aware of the situation. "I need two Type-1 crews and a chopper as soon as possible."

Spreading a map on the hood of his Forest Service truck, Scott scanned the area with his gaze before giving the coordinates to the dispatcher in the SO.

"We've got a crew stationed in Pine View and one in Evanston," she said.

"Roger. Get them to us as soon as you can."

"We'll do our best."

Scott signed off again and stowed his radio in his pants pocket. He'd need it handy over the next few hours. The fire was no more than five miles from Opal Ranch, followed by the Donaldson and Taylor ranches. Too close for comfort. If the wind changed, they'd be in trouble.

Scott whipped out his cell phone and dialed Melanie's number. The phone rang and rang, with no voice mail picking up. That was a bad sign that the phone lines were out. What if Melanie wasn't aware of the fire yet? She'd need time to move her sheep and he didn't dare leave to go and warn her.

It would take an hour before a pumper truck arrived and almost two hours for a hotshot crew. It seemed like a lifetime. To be on the safe side, they needed to move as much livestock as possible and evacuate the local ranchers. Just in case.

Scott faced Marty. "I believe we have a standing contract to use your crawler tractor to build fire line, right?"

"Yep. I can have one here in an hour. I'll stop by the Donaldsons' to see if Frank can also bring his tractor over," Marty said.

"That would be great. We have a standing contract with him, too. Can you stop by the McAllisters on your way? I'd like to warn Melanie about the fire."

Marty turned, but kept walking backward. "Their place is too far out. I need time to move some of my livestock."

Scott turned to the other man standing nearby. He didn't recognize him, but being new to town, Scott didn't know everyone yet. "What about you? Can you drive to the McAllisters' place and warn them?"

The father shrugged. "We're not from around here, mister. We were just driving through on our way to go see Zion's National Forest. If you can give us directions, we could probably find it."

"No, thanks. It would be best if you got going. In another hour, we may need to close the road." The last thing Scott wanted was tourists getting lost in the middle of a brush fire.

He breathed a sigh of relief when the family headed for their car, loaded up and took off.

While Marty ran to his vehicle and drove home, Scott returned to his truck and reached for his fire pack. During fire season, he kept it with him at all times. All forest rangers were trained wildfire fighters. He pulled on his Nomex pants with deep, baggy cargo pockets on the legs and hips. Next came his bright yellow, fire-resistant shirt-jacket and helmet. He clipped his goggles to his helmet, then removed his regular boots. With the truck door open, he sat on the seat and pulled on his heavy wildland fire boots with lug soles and nine-inch tops. Last and most importantly, he stowed his Nomex gloves inside his pocket, then strapped on a radio chest harness. No matter what, he carried his folded-up fire shelter on his back, but chose to leave his personal gear, sleeping bag, water and food rations in the truck.

Following the eighteen watchout situations, which included identifying escape routes, Scott remained on the road and waited. He kept busy, making calls to the Sheriff's Office and the high school principal to put them on alert. If he needed to set up an incident command center, the local high school was the best location. Fire crews could sleep, shower and eat there once they got a logistics chief to set it all up.

Scott tried calling Melanie's house and her cell phone, but she didn't answer. He regretted not having gotten her a satellite phone yet. Where could she be?

He called Marty Taylor's cell phone. He was over at the Donaldson place. "Frank said to tell you he'll have a tractor over there in about an hour."

Scott hid his surprise. With the fire so near their property, the Donaldsons had a lot at stake, but Scott still welcomed their willingness to pitch in. "I appreciate it."

Scott hung up his cell phone and glanced at his watch. With each passing minute, the fire ate up acres of dry grass and brush. By the time Marty and Frank arrived with their tractors, the fire perimeter had doubled in size.

Scott paced the roadside, waiting anxiously for his fire crew to show up. He set a limit on where the fire could get to before he got in his truck and drove to Opal Ranch to search for Melanie and the girls. They were probably outside with the sheep and Melanie had left her cell phone in the house or had it turned off. Rolling clouds of smoke choked the skies, sending flames high into the air. Surely Melanie could see and smell the fire. Although he didn't want to leave right now, he'd evacuate them himself before he'd allow the fire to hurt them.

Holding his radio two inches away from his mouth, he pressed the call button. "Ennison to Karen."

"This is Karen. Go ahead."

"Did you happen to hear from Melanie McAllister?"

"No, sir."

"I haven't been able to reach her and thought she might have contacted you."

"Negative."

"If she calls, let me know immediately."

"Roger. Do you want me to drive out to Opal Ranch and see if I can locate her?"

"No. It'd take you too long, and I need you in the office to coordinate things. I'll take care of it. Out."

Where was Melanie? She expected him for dinner and should be home. With everything he had going on here, he didn't want to worry about them right now. He wanted them where they would be safe.

A screaming siren caught Scott's attention and he turned to see Sheriff Chambers zipping down the narrow road. Two pumper trucks and a transport vehicle filled with fire crew followed.

Finally.

Within the hour, the area became a bee-hive of activity. Pumper trucks and tractors clogged the side of the road.

"What can I help with?" the sheriff asked.

"You can put some red cones along the road down there and direct traffic away from this place." Scott pointed toward the road leading to town. "The last thing we need is a bunch of rubberneckers getting in the way to see what's going on."

"You got it." The sheriff trotted toward his car.

A fire crew of twenty men and three women arrived wearing fire-resistant clothing and armed with shovels and Pulaskis, a special hand tool that combined an ax and an adze in one head. As the crew gathered around, Scott gave instructions.

"We'll anchor and flank it. Let's set the road as our anchor point. I don't want any crews out in front of the fire. The winds are moving too fast. We'll have to attack from the sides until we can get more manpower or a chopper to drop retardant on the front to slow the fire down. I think we can pinch it off on the sides."

The crew went to work digging trenches, using shovels and Pulaskis to scrape back grass, brush and other fuels.

"Karen told me some boys were sighted up here with a campfire," Jim Tippet said. "You think that's what caused this burn?"

Scott coughed against the smoke. "It's highly likely. Once we have the fire under control, we'll investigate the cause."

He wished he had a hotshot crew here. Smoke jumpers always got a lot of publicity, but no one built fire line faster than a skilled hotshot crew. Man for man, Scott would match an experienced and physically conditioned member of a hotshot crew with a smoke jumper any day. Hotshots ate small fires like this for breakfast.

Within two hours, the hotshots from Pine View arrived. Scott put a holding crew on one side to ensure the fire remained within prescribed boundaries. The Pine View crew worked the other side to squeeze off and contain the flames. It appeared they were making good headway. Three-man crews used hoses connected to two pumper trucks, spraying gushers of water at the flames. Steam rose from the fire, adding to the black cloud churning above. The smoke lingering over the roadway was so thick that drivers had to turn on their headlights.

Everything was working just fine. The static of radio traffic accompanied the whoosh of water from thick fire hoses. Gray smoke billowed over the mountain, the air heavy with the scent of burnt grass and sage.

The crews were fighting fire on two fronts. The fire spreading across the meadow, fanned by a breeze it created itself, and the fire heading toward the mountains, toward big timber.

They almost had it under control. The hotshot crew from Evanston would soon arrive and the added manpower would be all they needed to contain this fire. Scott figured he'd be home in time to tuck Shelley into bed that night.

And then the wind shifted east. Toward Opal Ranch.

Chapter Twelve

"Anne! Shelley! Where are you?" Melanie raced through the barn again, checking each animal stall, climbing up to search the hay-loft.

Nothing! Where were they?

She ran outside, checking each corral, scanning the hay fields with urgency. Smoke from the west filtered over the air, making her cough. She'd been so busy bottling beets that she hadn't noticed the smoke until she went to call the girls in to help make supper. There'd been no lightning storms and she couldn't determine where the fire came from. It must be manmade.

Fear roiled through her. She wouldn't leave the ranch without her girls.

"Bob! Here boy!" She whistled for the dog, but he didn't come. No doubt he'd gone with the girls, wherever that might be.

Jumping on a four-wheel quad, she started the engine and drove down by the pond.

Maybe the girls had gone there. With the water no more than knee-deep, the girls liked to catch pollywogs and pick fluffy willows to put in a vase on the kitchen windowsill.

The girls weren't at the pond. Panic climbed Melanie's throat, shutting off her air supply. Where were they? Oh, when she got hold of them, she'd give them a piece of her mind. Why had they gone off without telling her first?

Changing her tactics, she drove out to the fields. That effort proved fruitless and ate up twenty precious minutes. Common sense told her to find the girls and get out of here as fast as possible.

When she returned to the house, she checked the tool and lambing sheds. The girls could be anywhere, but they'd had a fight earlier. Shelley had finally gotten angry at Anne's insults about Scott being a ranger and told Anne off. Melanie had broken up several verbal fights that day and finally threatened that the girls wouldn't get to watch their movie tonight if they didn't stop arguing. So where had they gone? Were they together or separated?

It was time to call Scott. She didn't know what else to do. She couldn't find the girls.

Lost in thought, she rounded the corner

to the house and shrieked. "Scott! Oh, thank goodness you're here." Relief flooded her and she almost threw herself into his arms. She didn't need to. He wrapped his strong arms around her and pulled her close for a quick hug.

"I've been trying to call you for two hours. Where have you been?" His voice sounded clogged with emotion or soot. She wasn't sure which.

His presence brought her immediate comfort. With him here she knew everything would be okay. If they could just find the girls.

"I've been in the house. No one's called today." She drew back and took a good look at him. Black streaks marred his face and he wore a yellow helmet and firefighter garb.

"The phone lines are down."

"I didn't know," she said breathlessly.

"What about your cell phone?"

She pressed the palm of her hand against her forehead. "It's in the house, turned off. I figured if someone needed to reach me, they'd call my landline. I can't find the girls."

"What?" He blinked, his eyes red from smoke.

She quickly explained about the girls. "I've been frantic to find them."

"I've got to get you out of here. It's not safe anymore." He turned toward the garden, scanning the back fields for signs of life.

"Where could they be?"

His gaze moved over the thin road leading back to the south pasture and his brow furrowed. "You moved the lambs several days ago so they could graze, didn't you?"

"Yes." She paused. "No, they wouldn't. That's two miles away. Surely they wouldn't walk all that way just to see the lambs —" She couldn't finish. Her body prickled with alarm. "But that's closer to the fire."

"We're out of time. Get in your truck and meet me down there." He sprinted toward the tractor.

Anxious with worry, Melanie ran to the truck, started the engine and drove down the road. In her rearview mirror, she saw Scott following with the tractor at a slower pace and knew he planned to build fire line.

Was the fire really that close? Surely they had time to round up the lambs and herd them out of danger. If only she hadn't been working so intently inside the house and had seen the smoke sooner.

Her heart beat madly in her chest as she bounced along the rutted road, which was little more than a trail used only by her. She saw the smoke backlit by flame. The sheep were huddled in a far corner of the fenced pasture, milling around nervously. But where were the girls — ?

There! Relief flooded Melanie when she saw them among the sheep. Bob ran along the perimeter, tongue lolling out of his mouth as he urged the flock toward the fence. He'd done what he'd been trained to do. Move the sheep as far away from danger as possible.

Thick clouds of smoke filtered through the truck vents, making it difficult to breathe. Melanie stopped the truck and hopped out. She jumped the fence and dashed through the alfalfa toward the girls.

"Anne! Shelley!" she screamed at the top of her voice.

"Momma!" Anne cried.

Melanie scooped the two girls into her arms, kissing them both, scanning their faces for injuries. "Are you okay?"

"Yes, but I can't breathe," Anne said.

Shelley coughed, a thick hacking sound.

"Come on." Taking each of their hands, she ran toward the truck, half dragging the girls behind her. She would not let go no matter what.

Scott met them at the truck. Sitting on the tractor, he pointed toward the house in the distance. "Get them out of here right now."

"Can't we move the sheep?" Melanie shouted over the roar of the tractor engine.

"No time. Take care of our girls. Go! I'll protect the sheep." He looked toward the west and his eyes narrowed, as if he were calculating how much time he had before the flames engulfed him. And then he turned and did something that stunned Melanie and stopped her breath cold.

He stepped down off the tractor, pulled her close, and kissed her. Once. Quick and fierce. And then he was gone.

Waves of emotion trembled over Melanie's body. She couldn't let him go. She couldn't!

"No, Scott!" she cried. "It's not worth your life. Come with us. We won't leave you."

"Get going!" he yelled back as he settled into the driver's seat and shifted gears. The engine backfired as he pressed the accelerator and moved forward.

Melanie yelled for him to come back, but doubted he could hear above the engine. Stubborn, foolish man.

Watching him go, she stood there frozen. Helpless. Clasping the girls' hands like a lifeline. Fierce winds created by the fire whipped her long ponytail across her face.

"Daddy!" Shelley screamed for her father, tugging on Melanie's hand to run after him.

Melanie held firm. No matter what, she had to protect the children. She had to get them out of here.

Scott ignored them as he lowered the disk plow and drove along the outer edge of the pasture fence. The blade gouged up giant furrows of earth as he created a trail of fire line to protect the sheep.

"Melanie, please don't let him go," Shelley whimpered.

Even Anne jerked on Melanie's hand. "Mom! Make him come back."

Melanie couldn't do anything to stop him. There wasn't time. She had to trust Scott. She had to trust the Lord. Scott was an experienced ranger and firefighter and knew what he was doing. He trusted her to take care of their kids. To get them out of here safely.

She couldn't let him down.

"Come on, girls. Get in." She pulled them with her over to the truck and pushed them inside, then whistled for the dog. "Bob! Come!"

With a sharp bark, the dog came running and jumped inside, then Melanie closed the door. The animal panted and huddled with the girls on the seat.

As Melanie turned the truck to return to the ranch, she saw flames licking along the outer trail leading toward Simpson's Meadow. The sky above looked blood-red, surrounded by black smoke.

The girls swiveled in their seat, their noses pressed against the back window as they stared at Scott. Both of them sobbed, sniffing loudly. Shelley kept calling for her father, her pitiful cries shattering Melanie's heart into a thousand pieces.

"Daddy. Daddy."

Looking in her rearview mirror, Melanie shivered in spite of the tremendous heat. A wall of flame engulfed the area where the tractor had been and she prayed silently, harder than ever before in her life.

Please, God. Please don't take him from me now. Don't let him get hurt. Please let him live.

Oh, Scott! Her common sense told her he couldn't endure this. No matter how strong and self-assured he was, no man could survive this fire.

She couldn't lose Scott. Not now when she realized how much she loved him. She loved him even as she realized she'd lost him. And it was her fault. He may have lost his life saving their girls. Fighting to save Opal Ranch.

Her emotions overwhelmed her and she

wiped her eyes, trying to see through the blur of tears and smoke. Trying to be strong once more.

Please, Lord. Please don't take him from me now. Have mercy on us. Please.

The roar of fire filled Scott's ears, deafening him. All he heard was the pounding of his heart as the disk plow reached the end of fence and beyond. Ten, twenty, thirty yards.

Adrenaline pumped through his body. The fire circled and swirled before him. Pain embraced his body, the heat almost unbearable. Smoke clogged his lungs and he coughed violently. He had to protect his lungs from the hot air. Had to get inside his fire shelter.

One thought brought him solace. His girls were safe — all three of them. If he died today, they would live. His precious daughters and Melanie.

Then he felt a lance of doubt. He'd failed them. He had kept his promises to the ranchers, but not to his girls. He'd failed to protect Opal Ranch. Failed to keep his promise to Shelley that he'd never leave her.

What would happen to Shelley with him gone? Would Melanie look after his little girl? Would Melanie love and raise Shelley like her own? The thought of his innocent child being raised in foster homes nearly broke him.

And gave him the will to fight.

He couldn't outrun the fire. His best chance for survival was to ride it out. He might have one chance, if he hurried. Maybe —

Flames danced all around the perimeter he'd just created, so close he could spit at them. He jerked his face and neck shroud up to cover his nose, protecting his lungs from the toxic smoke. He killed the engine. As he scrambled off the tractor, he reached back for his fire shelter. Even through the Nomex gloves, his hands burned like they'd touched a hot stove.

He wasn't going to make it. He'd run out of time.

Don't think that! Keep going. Don't quit. Think of Shelley. Think of Melanie.

So much to live for. So much to love.

Through the black haze, he tried to find a spot well away from the grass, brush and other fuels. He tried to see through the haze of heat waves, looking so much like a mirage. The sound of the fire popping, crackling and sizzling seemed to taunt him. The flames snaked along the edge of the fence, coming closer. Seeking him out.

Tracking him.

His body pumped with adrenaline, but he still felt the pain. The blisters forming on his ears, hands and face. The stifling heat, so hot he could barely breathe.

Smoke stung his eyes and he blinked. His chest heaved as he gasped for air. His fingers fumbled with the red ring on his fire shelter. He pulled hard, then tore off the plastic bag. Clasping the handles, he shook furiously to unfold the shelter. The winds whipped it, trying to steal it away. He couldn't hold the shelter straight, but he gripped it like steel. Nothing would rip it out of his hands except death.

He'd made a promise to Anne. And to himself. He'd vowed to keep Opal Ranch safe. To protect Anne and Melanie, no matter what. To be there for Shelley.

He choked, knowing he may have failed in his promises, but he'd tried. So hard. He'd dallied too long, trying to save the orphan lambs. Trying to save the ranch.

Walls of flame surrounded him, closing in. Panic climbed up his throat, but he fought it off. Fought to follow the safety training ingrained in him over years and years of work and practice.

All he saw were flames and smoke, moving fast. So fast.

He was going to die, a horrible, painful death. He wasn't going to make it.

Not this time.

CHAPTER THIRTEEN

Melanie pulled into the yard at Opal Ranch and stared, her fingers gripping the steering wheel until her knuckles whitened. Firefighters dressed in yellow shirts, their faces black with filth, tromped through her fields and corrals. Pumper trucks, crawler tractors, engines and trucks filled the yard as men dug up her hay field to build fire line. Thank goodness Scott had already brought in the hay. He never dawdled and always took such good care of the ranch.

Thinking about him brought a fresh round of tears to dampen her smoke-burned eyes.

The girls sat on the seat and stared toward the meadow, their faces ashen with shock. They'd just watched a wall of fire engulf Scott and seemed to be in a daze.

Shocked with disbelief.

"You girls wait here. Don't move from this spot." Melanie got out and tried to run to Jim Tippet. She staggered, her legs trembling.

"Jim! Hurry!" She tried to yell, but her voice came out as a soft croak. Her throat burned with smoke.

"Where's Scott?" he asked.

She pointed, unable to contain the sobs shaking her body. "He's got my tractor there in the south pasture. He . . . he's trying to build fire line to protect the sheep. He's in danger. Please! Hurry!"

Clouds of smoke billowed around the south road, cutting the pasture off from view. The lambs and Scott were nowhere to be seen. Melanie covered her mouth with one hand, trying to stifle the sobs coming from her throat. Scott and the sheep must have been consumed by fire.

"Please help him."

Jim must have heard her weak plea as her knees sank beneath her. He caught her, his soot-covered face filled with anguish. "Scott's out there?"

She could only nod.

"Troy!" Jim yelled to another man who came running. "Take Mrs. McAllister and her children up to the house and stay with them. Get them out of here if we aren't able to contain the fire."

Troy nodded. "Will do."

Jim lifted his radio to his mouth and called

for Scott. "Tippet to Ennison, come in."

No response.

More urgently. "Tippet to Ennison, do you read me?"

A static void filled the airwaves with nothingness.

Jim headed toward a fire crew. Without breaking stride, he hollered orders. "Get on the phone to Evanston. I want an ambulance and chopper here right now. Don't take no for an answer. You men come with me."

Troy gathered up Anne and Shelley, doing the best he could to comfort the three sobbing females. Melanie didn't want to leave, but she must think of the girls. She couldn't do anything for Scott, but she could be there for Shelley.

As ordered, Troy led them all to the house, propping his Pulaski beside the back porch where Melanie refused to go any farther.

"We'll sit here on the porch swing," she croaked out.

She must have some damage to her lungs. She tried to take a deep breath, to settle her nerves, but ended up coughing. When she gained control again, she spoke to Troy. "Do you have a medic who can look at the children? They breathed in a lot of smoke and I want to make sure they're okay."

"Sure. I'll be right back." He gave her a

compassionate smile before trotting off to find someone.

Melanie sat on the back porch with Shelley and Anne, the three of them huddled together as they stared toward the south pasture. Melanie wrapped an arm around each girl and they all sobbed quietly.

Inconsolable. The pain was almost too much to bear.

The whap-whap of chopper blades beating overhead brought their heads up. They watched as the chopper flew low in the east, dropping its load of red retardant on the front of the fire. Melanie knew it would slow the progress of the flames so the ground crews could build fire line to protect the Donaldson and Taylor ranches. This wasn't the first wildfire she'd seen during her years as a rancher, but this was the closest she'd come to losing her ranch. And the first time she'd lost someone she loved to fire.

She trembled with shock and grief. She dreaded what the fire crew might find in the south pasture. Once they got over the disbelief, how could she explain to Shelley that her daddy wasn't coming back? How could she understand it herself? Everything had happened so fast, she didn't know what to think.

"It's my fault." Anne's voice sounded thin

with tears. "He promised to protect Opal Ranch and he did. But I didn't think he'd get ki-killed."

Melanie hugged the girls tighter, barely able to do more than whisper a reply. "It's no one's fault, sweetheart. He was doing his job, fighting to protect all of us."

"But . . . but why didn't he . . . come with us?" Shelley wept.

"He thought he could protect our lambs. He was giving us time to get away safely."

"Is Daddy dead?" Shelley asked.

"I don't know, sweetie." It did no good to pretend or to give false hope. Until Jim found Scott's body, Melanie refused to give up hope. Refused to believe such a strong, wonderful man could die so young.

Scott! Thinking of him brought a renewed ache to Melanie's heart. Tears streamed down her face. She couldn't brush them away. Her hands were busy holding the girls close. Trying to be strong while her entire world crashed down around her head. How could she stand to let Scott go?

"If Daddy dies, I'll be a full dogie. I won't have anyone." Shelley's voice sounded like a whimper.

"That's not true." Melanie pressed her damp cheek against the child's.

"You'll always have us," Anne said.

"That's true," Melanie agreed. "I love you so much, sweetheart. We want you always, don't we Anne?"

Anne sniffled, wiping her nose on the back of her sleeve as she nodded. "Sure, we . . . We're sisters. You can always st-stay with us. Forever."

"Even if I'm a ranger's kid?"

Anne nodded again. "I didn't mean it. Your dad's not a dirty rotten ranger. He's a rancher like us. Only a real rancher would fight so hard to save his flock."

"You're wrong, sweetheart. A real ranger fights just as hard," Melanie added.

In that instant, she realized that she loved Shelley. As much as she loved her own daughter. She couldn't help thinking about Christ's unconditional love for all mankind. A Bible verse in the book of John came to mind.

Greater love hath no man than this, that a man lay down his life for his friends.

Scott had done this for them. He had been willing to give his own life to save them. To give them time to flee to safety. To keep his promise and protect Opal Ranch.

No! He wasn't dead. He couldn't be. She refused to believe it. Not until she knew for sure.

"Shh," she soothed the two girls' tears.

"Let's just wait until Jim gets back, okay? Maybe your dad is fine and we're worrying for nothing. He knows how to fight wildfire. He's so good at everything he does. Let's just wait."

Silence overcame them then, but their anguish was palpable. A heavy, hollow emptiness filled Melanie. Common sense told her Scott could not have survived the blaze. And yet, she knew she must have faith. She must trust in the Lord and bend to His will.

She noticed the wind shifted again, blowing toward the south. Taking the stench of smoke with it. How she wished her broken heart could take wing as easily.

"Hey! What's that?" Anne pointed.

Through the haze of smoke shrouding the south road, a group of six men appeared, carrying a stretcher.

"Daddy!" Shelley bolted to her feet.

Melanie held onto the girl, not wanting her to see her father if he was badly burned or dead.

"Let me go! It's Daddy." The child squirmed to be free.

"Wait a minute, dear. Just wait."

As the men walked into the yard, Melanie saw a movement on the stretcher. A man's hand lifted and clasped Jim Tippet's arm.

Scott! He was alive.

But in what condition? Would he live? Even if he was scarred, Melanie couldn't help but love him with all her heart. She'd take him any way she could get him.

"Scott!" Anne took off at a dead sprint and Melanie could no longer hold Shelley back.

They all ran, pounding down the steps of the porch, racing across the yard like gazelles.

Shelley got there first. She was the fastest. "Daddy! Daddy!"

The firefighters set the stretcher on the loading dock by the barn, then cleared a path. Jim stood at Scott's head, grinning like a fool as he motioned for the medic.

Melanie stopped, looking at the man she loved.

Scott. He was alive. Here and now. Safe.

His bloodshot eyes were no more than white circles in a black canvas of soot. His eyebrows had been singed off, his hair damp with sweat. Shelley threw herself at him and he grimaced, then flashed a white smile. Anne stood back, smiling with uncertainty.

"Hi, babe." His voice sounded raw as he greeted his daughter.

Speaking set off a spasm of uncontrollable coughing. Acrid smoke must have burned

281

his lungs and throat. His clothing was covered with soot.

"Real gentle, sweetie." Jim tugged on Shelley's shoulders so she didn't hurt her father.

"Are all our crews okay?" Scott asked Jim.

"Yes, they're all fine."

Melanie couldn't believe that Scott's first concern was for his men. Her gaze quickly took in the damage. Small blisters dotted his face, ears and hands. His dear, calloused hands, which worked and served so willingly.

The burns would soon heal and weren't too serious. But what about his legs?

As an emergency technician examined him, she scanned Scott's limbs, searching for damage. Praying he'd be able to walk again.

He seemed to read her mind, speaking in a harsh whisper. "I'm gonna be fine. I just need some rest and to clear my lungs of smoke."

To prove his point, he bent his legs and wiggled his feet. His gaze met hers as she leaned against the dock and cupped his blackened cheek with her palm. He reached up and took her hand, drawing it to his mouth where he pressed a long kiss against her knuckles. His eyes closed, as if savoring the kiss. Her heart melted.

"Don't you ever do that again, Scott Ennison. No flock of sheep or building is worth your life. Not to me." She gazed into his eyes, loving him. Filled with so much joy she could hardly contain it.

"The flock is safe." His hoarse voice sounded so alien. So different from the rich timbre she adored. "They huddled together in the farthest corner of the pasture and didn't budge. The fire didn't reach them at all, but they may need help with their lungs."

"We'll get them checked out as soon as we can."

Shelley flashed a smile at Anne. "Did you hear that? Daddy saved our lambs."

"Thanks, Scott. Thanks for keeping your promise," Anne said.

"You're welcome."

Melanie stepped back, giving the medic room to work. Within ten minutes, they'd moved Scott into the house where they had better access to water. The medic gave Scott oxygen, then pulled up his sleeve, wrapped a tourniquet around his arm and hooked up an IV of fluids.

"Here, hold this." The medic handed the IV bag to Jim, then wrapped a blood pressure cuff around Scott's upper arm. He cleaned Scott's more serious wounds, bandaged his hands and put salve on his other burns.

"I'd feel better if that ambulance got here. Maybe I should drive you to Evanston myself," Jim said.

"In a few minutes, Jim. First, I need to talk to my girls." Scott's voice sounded stronger, although he continued to cough.

With so many firefighters tromping through her house, Melanie spread old sheets and towels across her furniture and carpets to protect them from being stained. Jim hovered close by with the IV bag as Scott lay on the kitchen table and looked at Melanie and their two daughters. He smelled like burnt popcorn and looked like death warmed over.

"Why did you two go out to the south pasture?" he asked the girls.

Shelley took a shallow breath. "We saw the smoke and wanted to make sure our lambies were okay."

Melanie shook her head. "But why did you go without telling me?"

"You wouldn't have let us go," Anne said.

Children thought in such simple terms. If the girls had told Melanie about the smoke, she might have been able to do something sooner.

"We had to check on our lambs," Anne

284

continued. "Mom told us the story of the Good Shepherd in Sunday school. Jesus left 999 sheep just to go check on one lost lamb."

"It wasn't quite 999," Melanie said.

Shelley wrapped her arms around her father and leaned her cheek against his chest. "We have a whole bunch of sheep to check on, so we figured they were really important."

Melanie chuckled. What else could she do? If she didn't laugh, she'd cry. "I think you got the gist of the story a bit wrong."

"They got it right. We've raised two soft-hearted girls and I wouldn't have it any other way." Scott's eyes crinkled at the corners, showing thin creases of white flesh where the soot hadn't reached him. "But don't go check your sheep in the middle of a range fire ever again without telling us first. Okay?"

Both girls nodded, their eyes filled with true remorse.

"I'm sorry, Scott." Anne's eyes filled with tears. "You almost got killed because of your promise to me."

"No, honey. I almost got killed because I'm a firefighter. This wasn't your fault. In fact, your mother will have to bear most of the blame for my survival."

"What?" Melanie cocked her head, not understanding. She thought she'd almost caused his death.

"I found myself surrounded by fire and saw no way out. I knew I was about to die. And then I remembered what you'd said about prayer. About the Lord being there for us anywhere, at any time. So I tried it. One last time."

He coughed long and hard and Melanie wondered if it was because of the smoke or the emotion filling his eyes. She and Jim both reached to help him outside. "We need to get you to the hospital, Scott."

He lifted a bandaged hand. "Not yet. I need to say something else while I can still bear to remember what happened out there today. Tomorrow, I plan to forget everything . . . except my Heavenly Father." He met Melanie's eyes. "I thought I was a goner. So I prayed for the first time in two years, as I've never prayed before. And right then, the wind shifted south, whipping the fire away from me." Coughing again, he struggled to continue. "The flames were so close I could reach out and touch them. But when the wind shifted, I was able to get inside my fire shelter and wait it out. I kept praying and didn't move until Jim found me."

Jim patted Scott gently on the shoulder, his eyes slightly damp. This was an emotional time, even for big, strong firefighters.

"Let's go to the hospital," Jim said.

"Scott, I . . . I . . ." Anne stepped near, her eyes filled with penitent tears.

He smiled and reached for her with his bandaged hands. With a hollow sob, the girl launched into his arms, missing his grimace of pain. He didn't say a word, but held the girl close for several moments. Melanie could just make out her whispered apology.

"I'm so sorry." Anne's shoulders trembled. "For everything. For being rude and saying you were a dirty rotten ranger. I'm so glad you're okay."

He closed his eyes tight and turned his face so he could kiss her hair. "It's okay, Anne. Shh. Don't cry, honey. Everything's gonna be all right. I'm glad you and your mother are okay, too."

He opened his eyes and met Melanie's gaze. She found herself brushing tears away from her cheeks again. This had been a difficult day. All it took to center one's priorities was a life-threatening catastrophe. Nothing else mattered in the world except the people she loved.

Scott released Anne, then stood as Jim steadied him. Melanie hated to let him go.

Hated to lose sight of him. What if he were more injured than they believed? She'd heard of lung damage taking a person's life following a forest fire. But right now, in front of these people, wasn't the time to tell him how she felt about him. And yet, she might never get another chance.

"Scott, I —"

The medic bolted through the door. "A chopper just arrived to fly Mr. Ennison to Evanston."

Two paramedics rushed inside and aimed their sights on Scott. Within moments, they whisked him out the door toward the helicopter parked in the front yard. Shelley stayed right beside her dad. Melanie and Anne followed.

Most of the firefighters had left, moving to the east where they would maintain the fire until it burned itself out. Jim had assigned one crew to clean up at Opal Ranch, to ensure that the fire in Melanie's fields was really out. Ash blanketed every available surface, turning the front lawn to gray. Melanie almost laughed. What did a little ash matter when the man she loved was safe and she'd see him again tomorrow?

Tomorrow! It seemed like forever. Melanie hated to let Scott go.

Frank Donaldson and Marty Taylor stood

at the bottom of the porch steps, waiting to greet Scott. At Scott's urging, the medics paused for just a moment.

Frank held his beat-up cowboy hat with his plump, blunt fingers. His face flushed with humility. Melanie stood close by, finding it ironic to see such a large, tall man looking so ashamed.

Frank reached out to shake Scott's hand. The man stuttered and shifted his weight with discomfort. "I . . . I heard what you did, Mr. Ennison. I just want to say I'm sorry for all the trouble my family and I caused you. No other ranger's ever kept his promise to us." He swallowed hard. "I didn't know what kind of man you were until today. I'm sorry. You won't have any more trouble from me or my family."

"Call me Scott. And apology accepted." Scott nodded but didn't smile.

Melanie wondered how he continued to be so gracious. Surely he must be in tremendous pain. In spite of everything, he'd offered his forgiveness. How lucky she was to have such a man in her life. She didn't want to lose him. Didn't want him to leave.

"I also owe you a debt of gratitude," Marty said. "If you hadn't plowed that fire line across Melanie's south pasture, the fire would have burned right through and come over the hill to my place. I can't thank you enough for stopping it in time."

So finally the other ranchers had seen what a good man Scott Ennison really was.

A man who kept his promise.

As she watched the medics help Scott and Shelley into the chopper, Melanie wished she could go with them. The blades whirred overhead, blowing dust around the yard.

She had to stay here, to take care of her sheep. She wasn't Scott's wife. She hadn't even told him she loved him and she had no right to tag along.

Tomorrow, she'd go see him, even if it meant making a trip to the hospital in Evanston. Even if it meant driving to the ends of the earth. Somehow she must find the courage to tell him how she really felt. To ask him to stay in Snyderville. With her. Forever.

She just hoped he would agree.

CHAPTER FOURTEEN

Scott showed up on Melanie's doorstep with Shelley at eight o'clock the next morning. Dressed in his best Sunday suit, he'd taken extra care with his appearance, but figured he still looked pretty rough around the edges. Though they would soon heal, red burns and blisters dotted his neck and ears. When Melanie opened the front door, Scott felt such a sense of relief. Seeing her did something to him inside, making him giddy with happiness.

"Scott!" Her eyes widened in surprise and her gaze swept over his attire. "What are you doing here?"

"I don't mean to intrude, but can I speak with you and Anne for a few minutes?"

She pushed the screen door wide. "Of course. Don't be silly. You're always welcome here. Come in . . . please."

He caught the joyful lilt in her voice, the sound soothing his jangled nerves like water to a parched throat. A lance of hope speared him. What he was about to do required quite a bit of courage and he needed all the encouragement he could get.

"Anne!" Melanie called to the back of the house. "Scott and Shelley are here."

Anne came running, wearing her blue jeans and pajama top, as if she'd been in the middle of changing her clothes. "Shelley!"

The two girls hugged and Scott realized they'd formed a bond few real sisters ever enjoyed. They'd reconciled their differences over being a rancher and ranger.

Melanie gestured to the recliner. "Sit down, Scott. Are you sure you should be out of the hospital already? How are your lungs? What did the doctor say?"

He chuckled, enjoying her worrying about him. It had been a long time since a woman cared enough to ask if he was okay and he couldn't explain why it meant so much to him now.

Because he loved her. That's all he knew for certain anymore. And he loved the Lord. Until yesterday, he didn't realize how much he'd missed God in his life.

"I'm fine. I have a clean bill of health. The doctor said my lungs are strong, though I may have a cough for a while. Otherwise,

I'm good."

She sat across from him while the girls plopped back on the couch. Their smiles were contagious. They needed to celebrate the gift of life.

"That's amazing," Melanie said. "I can't believe what you went through and yet you're okay. The Lord really did bless us yesterday."

"Yes, He did," Scott agreed. "And I'm hoping He'll bless me again today."

She tilted her head. "How so?"

He slid to his knees and reached out to gently take each of their hands into his larger, bandaged hands. Even Shelley stared in confusion.

"Dad?"

"Shh."

They scooted close together and he looked into each of the little girls' eyes, before finally locking gazes with Melanie.

Melanie gasped. "Scott, you —"

"Shh. Just listen for a moment and then you can talk all you want."

She bit her bottom lip, looking so vulnerable that he felt the strong urge to kiss her.

He gripped her hand, trying not to squeeze too hard. "I can't tell you what the past few months have meant to me, working here at Opal Ranch, watching Shelley come to love Anne like a real sister. I know we've never formally dated, but I don't need a night out on the town to know how I feel about you. No restaurant or movie theater could ever compete with the sunsets we've shared." A lump rose to his throat, but he forged ahead. "I never thought I'd find love again, but I have. It's here at Opal Ranch. If the girls agree, I want us to be a real family. I love you, Melanie. I love you and Anne."

Melanie's eyes welled up. "Oh, Scott . . ." she whispered.

"I didn't mean for this to happen. In fact, loving you poses all sorts of problems for us," he admitted ruefully. "But love isn't convenient. It's something that takes hold of our hearts and makes us better people. My love for you has made me whole again."

Tears of joy rolled down her cheeks. "Scott, you've made so many promises to me, to the girls and to the other ranchers. And you've kept every one of them. But I'm afraid I need to ask for one more promise from you."

"What's that?" Now that he'd gotten the words out, his voice cracked like an adolescent boy. If she refused him, he'd be crushed.

"Promise to stay here with me always and love me forever. Because . . ."

"Because?" he urged.

"Because I love you, too. I was frantic when I thought you might be gone. Please stay with me always."

His heart beat rapidly and he longed to take her in his arms. But he needed to hear one more thing.

He turned to look at Anne. "Honey, would you mind being real sisters with Shelley? No one will ever take the place of your father, but would you mind if I were your new dad?"

Anne's brow furrowed. "You mean for keeps?"

"Yes, for keeps."

"And you'd live here at Opal Ranch with Mom and me? And I'd have to share my room with Shelley?"

He released a shuddering sigh, praying she agreed. "Yes, that's what I mean."

The girl hesitated, then her face lit up with a smile brighter than the Fourth of July. "Sure! Shelley will be my real sister and it's a good thing."

"Why is that?" Melanie asked with a laugh.

"Because then Scott won't be a full ranger. He'll be a half rancher, which isn't quite as bad. And Shelley and I won't be half dogies anymore. We'll both have a mom and a dad."

Scott chuckled, amazed at the child's reasoning.

Shelley nodded. "I like that plan. I wouldn't mind being a rancher and living here at Opal Ranch."

The girls hugged each other, hopping up and down.

"Scott."

Melanie drew his attention and he couldn't believe the love he saw shining in her eyes.

He came to his feet and sat beside her on the couch, cupping her hand in his. "I'm sorry I don't have an engagement ring for you yet. I was hoping you and the girls might like to drive into Evanston with me this afternoon to pick one out. If you'll have me."

The girls paused, staring at Melanie expectantly.

"Say yes, Mom. Say yes!" Anne urged.

Shelley grinned. "If you say yes, then Anne and I get to be bridesmaids."

A happy giggle escaped Melanie's throat. "Yes! Yes! I can't fight all of you. Of course, yes."

"All right!" Scott scooped her into his arms, kissing her lips, holding her close.

The girls joined them in a family bear hug. The room filled with happy laughter as they all discussed what this change might mean in their lives.

"It means Scott will be a half rancher," Anne said.

"It means I'll have a new sister," Shelley added.

Melanie's eyes sparkled. "It means I get to spend forever with the love of my life."

Scott kissed her again, then drew back slightly, their noses touching. "It means I get to keep another promise to my new family."

"Family." The word whispered past Melanie's lips on a sigh. "There isn't a better word in the English vocabulary."

As Scott held her tight, he couldn't agree more.

Dear Reader,

As we travel through life, we sometimes encounter people who for some reason don't like us. First as children, we may meet other kids on the playground or in high school whom we have a natural aversion to. Later in life, we may have neighbors, family members or business associates we don't get along with. No matter what the reason, the Lord expects us to seek peace. That doesn't mean we should let other people take advantage of us. Contention is not of God and we should look at ourselves to determine if we are part of the problem, or part of the solution.

In *The Forest Ranger's Promise,* both the heroine and the hero learn this lesson the hard way. According to the Gospel of Matthew, we must love our enemies and bless and pray for them that hate or persecute us. This can be particularly difficult when it affects our livelihood or family relationships. The Lord has not asked us to just get along with our enemies, but to actually love them. This is a higher law that requires a humble heart and lots of prayer to help overcome the anger or hatred we might feel toward some people. But like the Good Samaritan, we must obey God's law, not man's law.

I hope you enjoy reading *The Forest Ranger's Promise* and I invite you to visit my website at www.LeighBale.com to learn more about my books.

May you find peace in the Lord's words!

Leigh Bale

QUESTIONS FOR DISCUSSION

1. In *The Forest Ranger's Promise,* Scott Ennison is a forest ranger and Melanie McAllister is a sheep rancher. Their priorities for the use of our national forest lands sometimes differ and conflict. Some of the ranchers in their community hate Scott before they even know him. Have you ever disliked someone simply because of their profession? Have other people disliked you before they got to know you? How can you find ways to bridge these gaps of misunderstanding?

2. Scott Ennison believes his career choice as a forest ranger living in remote towns was partly responsible for the end of his first marriage. Even though he loved his profession, he was willing to give it up to save his marriage. Which is more important, a person's career choice or their marriage? Do you believe Scott changing his

profession choice would have made a difference in his marriage?

3. The apostles of Jesus included humble fishermen, a physician and a tax collector. Tax collectors were not considered very popular at that time. Did the Lord judge people based on their occupation? Or did He consider a person's actions, heart and mind to be more important?

4. Melanie helped Scott after he was injured, knowing she might be ridiculed by the other ranchers in her community. Have you ever been a Good Samaritan and helped someone in need even though you feared other people might not approve? Likewise, has anyone helped you when you felt like you didn't deserve their aid?

5. A woman caught in adultery was brought to Jesus for judgment and He said, "Neither do I condemn thee: go, and sin no more." How can we be more like Jesus in not judging our fellow man?

6. Anne was the child of a sheep rancher. Because of things her father had said and done, she hated all forest rangers. She frequently repeated labels and biases she

had learned from her dad. How can we keep from transmitting our own anger and biases to our children?

7. Following his painful divorce, Scott turned his back on God and refused to pray. In spite of losing her husband, Melanie came to depend more on God for support. Have events in your life caused you to turn away from the Lord? Or did you draw nearer to Him in prayer? Why or why not?

8. During Sunday school, Melanie had taught her daughter the story of the ninety-and-nine when the Savior went to search for the one lost lamb. Later, during the range fire, the little girls went to check on their orphan lambs, to ensure they were okay. Have you ever had the opportunity to visit people who are "lost" in the Gospel of Jesus Christ? Can we ever give up on these children of God?

9. When Donaldson's grocery store refused to sell food to Melanie because she was tending the forest ranger's daughter, she was forced to drive ninety miles to another town to buy food. This created an extra expense and burden on Melanie. Should

she have refused to tend the ranger's daughter? Why or why not? Have you ever had to go out of your way to help another person you esteemed your enemy?

10. Have you ever seen another person being treated unfairly by someone else? Did you intervene or remain silent? Why or why not?

11. Melanie's house was vandalized and her child terrorized because she was associating with the new forest ranger. She decided to press charges against the vandals. Have you ever been the target of a bully? How did you react? Do you believe Melanie made the right choice to press charges against these bullies? Or do you think she should have quit tending the forest ranger's daughter?

12. When the wildfire would have destroyed the homes of two ranchers who had been unkind to him, Scott continued to fight to protect their lands. When he found his own life in jeopardy, Scott turned to the Lord in prayer. Have you ever found yourself running out of options and turning to the Lord for help? Did God answer your prayer in a way you expected? Does

the Lord always answer our prayers in our time frame and in the way we expect?

13. When Melanie believed Scott may have been killed in the wildfire, she realized how much she loved and depended on him. At that point, she did not care what Scott's profession was. Have you ever had a defining event occur in your life that made you realize what is really important to you? Did this event change or reaffirm your priorities? If so, how?

14. At the end of the story, Frank Donaldson, the main rancher who has persecuted Scott and Melanie the most, approaches Scott and apologizes for what he has done. What brought about this change in Frank's attitude? How should we deal with people who refuse to change their hard hearts? Should Scott have accepted or refused Frank's apology? Why or why not?

ABOUT THE AUTHOR

Leigh Bale is a multiple award-winning author of inspirational romance, her awards including the prestigious Golden Heart. She holds a B.A. in history with distinction and is a member of Phi Kappa Phi Honor Society. A member of Romance Writers of America, Leigh also belongs to the American Christian Fiction Writers and various chapters of RWA, including the Faith, Hope and Love chapter and the Golden Network. She is the mother of two wonderful adult children and lives in Nevada with her professor husband of twenty-nine years. When she isn't writing, Leigh loves playing with her beautiful granddaughter, serving in her church congregation and researching another book. Visit her website at www .LeighBale.com.